Werewolf Apocalypse

&

Other Short Stories

by Michelle Rumple

For Brayden-Kai,

who never shies away from watching a horror flick with me

&

For Una, Jonathon, and Kiva

my three amigos

who flood me with all the serotonin I need to keep writing.

Contents

Introduction..............................5

Werewolf Apocalypse....................7

The Northern Triangle..................14

Deep in the Blue........................35

Survivor One............................53

Teddy Bear..............................60

Area 51.................................73

What in Deer Nation?..................100

Snow Storm............................137

Introduction

I love writing short stories because it's *like* writing a novel but without all the commitment and tears and do-overs. I have been writing short stories since elementary school but this collection, all written within the last few years, are very different from those early writing days.

This collection is meant to be horror though horror is different for everyone. I hope, within these short pages, that you, friend reader, find something to make you double-check the corners of your room. If not, I hope you at least enjoy them because they were really fun to write.

Werewolf Apocalypse

Elana felt the tears rolling down her cheeks, but she kept her trembling lips shut tight. A single sound, she knew, would lead her into frenzied panic and then she would surely never find her way out of the deep woods she had so foolishly ventured into.

Night had fallen fully though strangely there was plenty of light to see by. Elana knew she should stop moving, should find somewhere to spend the rest of the night and wait for daylight to try and find her way home. But she was terrified and movement kept her from sinking into the despair that gripped her.

Ahead, the trees thinned out and a few more steps brought her to a wide clearing flooded with moonlight. She stumbled forward, glad to be out of the thick darkness of the trees and collapsed against the side of a fallen tree that hung out over a cheerfully babbling stream. In the bright light of the full moon glowing overhead, Elana let herself utter a single, despairing sob. A voice above shocked her to the core and she whirled, stretching her neck up to see who spoke.

"Did you come here to see the moon as well?"

A wolf was lounging on the tree, stretched out for maximum comfort and for a moment, Elana was so flabbergasted that she couldn't quite figure out what she was seeing. And then pants came into focus and what looked like a soft vest and she realized it was a werewolf. That was when the scream that she'd been barely keeping under wraps burst forth, shattering the peace of the moonlit glade. The werewolf looked at her, lips pursed on its muzzle and it sucked its teeth at her. Elana let the scream die away into silence and pressed her own lips tightly together.

"Are you alright now?"

"Yes, sorry," she said, voice trembling.

"That's alright, I gather you've gotten lost and haven't come to see the moon at all."

"No, I mean yes. Er—I'm lost, but the moon is lovely and any other time…" She trailed off but the wolf nodded knowingly.

"I've been lost a time or two. Not in the woods, necessarily, I *am* a wolf, after all, but in life. So, I can relate. The screaming does seem to help a bit."

"Yes, quite," Elana clasped her hands together, afraid and confused and thinking that she might die in these woods after all.

"You're only a mile from your village, you know. Well, I assume it's your village. The only one around, after all. You just have to follow this stream and you'll be at the gates in no time."

"Really?" Elana breathed, relief flooding her and driving the fear out in an instant. She turned with a beaming smile but it dropped from her face as she saw that it had stood and was looking down at her, its face in shadow even in the brightness of the moon.

"I'll give you a head start, girl, but you'd better run now. The moon always makes me so hungry."

Elana gaped up at the wolf and watched in horror as saliva began to drip from its muzzle. It crouched down, leaned forward, and barked in her face. That was all she could take; Elana turned and fled, the wolf's laughter echoing behind her. Branches and bushes tore at her clothes and she hauled the bundles of her dress into her arms to free her legs, running as she'd never done before. Breath tearing in her throat, Elana felt the forest floor flying by under her feet and, just when the cramp in her side began to be very worrisome, she saw flashes of torches through the trees. She desperately wanted to scream for help, to have the villagers meet her halfway, but she needed every ounce of air to breathe, and she was close. *So* close to safety. The edge of the trees came into view, the line thinned where it met the open meadow that had been cleared back from the wall and Elana felt a laugh of relief bubble in her throat.

"Almost made it," a voice whispered in her ear and she was slammed to the side, a muzzle full of teeth punching into her gut. Elana pulled in one final breath and shrieked into the night, even as she died.

"I don't know why they even try," one guard said as the scream echoed out of the tree line toward them. The other guard shook his head, disgusted and deflated by the world and the death.

"We were supposed to have zombies. Slow, idiotic zombies that you could just fast-walk away from. What asshole started the Werewolf Apocalypse? Who had the brilliant idea, you know?" The first guard spit over the wall as he adjusted his rifle.

"I want to know who keeps telling people about this place. No one can get through the woods, it's crawling with those fuckers. So why do they keep trying?"

"It must be worse out there than we thought."

"It's exactly as bad as I thought, I remember the early days. Just because they can talk now and wear clothes doesn't make them any less brutal."

"Well, whatever. All I know is my shift is over in two hours and nothing has crossed the meadow. As long as those dogs stay in the woods, I don't give two goddamns about them."

The two guards laughed in the world-weary way of survivors who have nearly given up. Their world was over, the end brought about by an experiment that had gone horrifically wrong. In the woods, eyes shining with moonlight over a muzzle coated in blood watched the two men. Those eyes knew the time was coming. Those eyes knew there would be more blood soon.

The Northern Triangle

"Meers, it's not here. We've been in this Godforsaken wilderness for six weeks and I want to get back to my bed and my shower, okay? I don't even care about the research anymore."

"You're full of shit, Peters. Your life is meaningless without research, and everyone knows it. Look, we have this last valley and then we'll call it, alright? Another week, *tops*, and then we'll hang it up."

Peters groaned but stepped closer to the moss-covered stump that Meers had set their well-worn and heavily marked map on. The area was small compared to the massive area they and the rest of the team had already covered, and he knew Meers was right. A week would be more than enough time to search the area and, based on historical surveys, this small stretch hadn't been fully explored yet. Peters' fingers began itching for his gear and when he saw Meers smirking, he snorted and turned away.

"We have time to move the camp today. I'll head back and get the packing started, let the others know what's going on. We can be ready to start surveys in the morning."

Peters nodded and folded their map before heading toward the mouth of the valley to scout a good spot to set up their base camp. It was a fairly large outfit, as university outfits went, and he had seen a rocky stream nearby that he was sure would have a clear area large enough for everything they'd brought.

It was summer in Alaska but this close to the valley, the air was very cold, and Peters zipped his heavy jacket a little tighter as he hiked toward where he knew the stream was running. It was only just after one in the afternoon and the sun was high and bright overhead. Peters had only hiked ten minutes before he reached the stream and, just ahead of where he stood, he could see a large, flat area that would be perfect for their tents and equipment. He tied an orange ribbon on one of the short trees in the area and was turning to head back when slight movement in the valley below caught his attention. Peters turned quickly and saw the very edge of a large shadow moving behind what looked like the remains of an old rockslide. He squinted down at the area, trying to see better, but there was no further movement. Shrugging, he told himself to let the guide know to unpack the big gun. They had been no stranger to bears on this field expedition and while they'd been lucky in their encounters to this point, he knew the wildlife could be unpredictable this far from human civilization. The further into the interior they got, the less scared of them the animals were.

Peters met the rest of the team as they were driving up in the ATV's. Peters once again thanked the university gods for granting him as much money as they had; without the extra funding, they would never have been able to afford the vehicles. He was glad to be done with cobbled together research expeditions, held together with grit and duct tape. If this valley didn't pan out, then this expedition was as dead as his career.

He waved the group to follow him and led them back to the cleared area where they went to work setting up the camp. The interns and his research assistant began hauling out their equipment and everything to get dinner going. For once, Peters was ready to go to bed so that they could get as early a start as possible. Meers walked toward him, bringing the sampling kits.

"Peters, let's get these sorted so we have everything ready to go tomorrow. We'll have to be quick to get through the whole valley, but I want to make sure we don't make any mistakes." Peters nodded, though the implication that he would make a mistake rankled at him. Together they quickly inventoried the field sampling kits, replacing anything that was missing or damaged. It was a quick process and Meers took them to one of the ATVs to store it for the morning. While the guide and Peters' assistant got dinner ready, Peters walked to edge of the path that would lead them down into the valley. It was little more than an animal track but the way was clear and free of big debris which would allow the vehicle easy access to the bottom. He looked out over the relatively small valley below, noting the short trees, the wide meadow, and the rockfall at one end that looked old, with grass and moss covering the rocks. That was where he had seen the shadow, the bear, and he reminded himself again to let their guide know.

Once they'd eaten, the rest of the evening passed quickly, and Peters was in his tent, ready to sleep not long after. He thought again of the work that still lay ahead of them and the little time they had left. Despite his racing mind and the stress of what they may or may not find within the next week, Peters fell asleep quickly.

Screams woke him and, because it was still light out, Peters had no notion of what time it was or how long he'd been asleep. The effect was intensely disorienting and for several long moments all he could do was blink heavily, propped up on one arm. When the screaming started again and the sounds of frantic activity and voices in the camp outside erupted, Peters hurried to pull boots and a coat on despite his confusion. He stepped out of his tent and ran to where the others were standing near the edge of the valley, huddled close as they stared down.

"What is it? What's happened?" he asked Meers who was leaning slightly forward as he strained to see.

"I've no idea. I heard screams, they moved past my tent as though the person was running. When I came out of my tent, they were coming from down there." He pointed down into the dark shadows of the valley and when Peters peered down, he experienced a sickening doubling of his vision, almost vertigo, though it passed quickly.

"Well, who's missing? Did someone have a nightmare and wander off?" Everyone looked around, counting and matching faces and the confusion of the group deepened when they all realized that everyone was accounted for.

"It's the koosteka," one of the grad students said, his voice low and scared. Their guide snorted and looked at the student with scorn.

"It's 'Kushtaka'," he said with derision, "and we are too far north for that. Also, they prefer deeper waters than this tiny stream."

"*Also,*" Meers chimed in, "they are a folktale, not real."

"Okay, let's relax," Peters said, holding up his hands at the guide and grad student who were glaring at each other. "Maybe it's an animal, a bird or something. There's no one besides us for hundreds of miles so if we're all here, then it has to be something like that. Right?" He looked around, eyebrows raised as he dared anyone to voice what they were all thinking, even himself though he would never admit it. Alaska was vast, much of it unexplored, and it was anyone's guess what lurked in the hidden spaces of the wilderness.

"Okay, a bird then. Everyone agrees?" Meers looked around and then yawned hugely, ignoring the scared looks of the grad students. "I'm tired, it's the middle of the night, let's call it a bird and get to sleep. We have a month of work to do in a week's time so as soon as my alarm goes off, everyone is getting up. Good? Good. Nighty night." Turning his back on the now silent valley, Meers went back to his tent, shrugging his coat off as he crawled back in. Peters did the same after another glance at the others. He snuck one more quick glance back down at the valley but nothing darted across his vision, nothing screamed out, all was silent and still. He waited until he was sure the others were going back to their tents before crawling back into his own and zipping his sleeping bag all the way up around his ears. Despite being certain that he would be awake for some time after the commotion, Peters was asleep in seconds.

In the valley below, all remained silent, yet dozens of pairs of eyes watched the lip of the valley from the heavy shadow. Waiting.

All through the next day, the sounds of excavation, digging, and rock being moved and collected rang through the valley. Meers and Peters, eager to find any evidence, no matter how minor, of what they'd come to Alaska looking for, were driving their team into the dirt. Breaks were few and short, food was eaten standing and then the eaters were hustled back to work. The grad students did their fair share of grumbling, yet they were excited as well and, if not quite as eager as their mentors, eager enough to be a part of a discovery as potentially world changing as what they were there for. And so, despite the constant barrage from the two PhD's, they worked hard all day. It was nearing nine o'clock at night when an excited voice shouted out near the far side of the valley. Peters, Meers and the others dropped what they were doing and ran to where one of the grad students was frantically waving them over. Peters reached her first and when he looked down to where she pointed, he felt such a rush of elation that he would have blacked out had Meers not been there to steady him.

"We found it," Meers breathed. Around them, the students, guide and hired help all crowded around and looked down into a dip in the valley floor. The grad student had set up a lantern to work by and it illuminated the rock face that she'd uncovered. Peters and Meers followed behind as she led them down, the others at their heels, until they stood in front of a slab of stone that was half buried in the loose dirt of the valley floor. It was canted slightly to the left, but they could easily see the eerie designs that swirled over the dark stone. Meers clutched at Peters as the two of them dropped to their knees in front of the stone. Behind them, the grad student who had found it was taking careful pictures of every visible space. Meers reached his fingers out and brushed them along the designs, following the swirls and dots of patterns.

"What is it?" the guide asked, his voice full of wonder and, Peters noted, a small tinge of fear.

"A guide stone. One of three discovered in the last decade. Well, four now, including this one."

"A guide stone to what?"

"A doorway, a portal. To another world, if we're lucky." Peters stood and helped Meers to his feet. "We'll need all of the equipment moved here. I want to get started unburying it right away."

"It's nearly time to quit, though," one of the laborers said but stepped back when Peters whirled on him.

"Not for me it's not. Not for Meers or our grad students. Bring the equipment and then you are free to go back up to the campsite." The laborer looked from Peters to the guide who nodded slightly and then he and the others went to do as they were told.

"You're not going to open this doorway, are you?" their guide asked, eyeing the stone warily now.

"No, we need to get it back to our lab, study it in greater detail. The clues are here, no one has yet unlocked them, however." Meers turned back to the stone after he finished explaining while Peters went to supervise the equipment placement. The hired help moved quickly. Though they were working under the midnight sun, the valley was quickly filling with shadow. Each of the grad students grabbed lanterns and set them up around the small dip that held the stone, creating a bright, halo of light against the shadow. Once finished, the laborers hurried back to the winding trail that would lead them back up to the tents. The guide was the last to go. He watched as Peters and

Meers directed the students on how to dig out the buried base of stone, both men digging in to help, before he turned away. As he hurried to the trail, a flash of motion caught his attention along the far wall of the valley and he stopped to see if it would come again. He pulled his rifle into his hands and waited, wondering if a bear had found a cave down in this space. The movement, however, did not repeat itself so he shrugged and hurried up to find dinner and his tent. For tonight, these men and women were on their own, no matter the fee he'd been paid.

At the stone, the small group worked feverishly. Despite the lantern light, the shadows steadily deepened until, looking up, Peters realized they were a tiny island of light in a sea of darkness. A shiver of fear ran down his spine, but he shook it off and went back to the stone. They had reached the base and were carefully testing how much further would have to be dug out. Several of the students were attaching heavy straps to the top and middle of the stone to prevent it from toppling should they dig too much. So far, though, it seemed to be holding.

Peters was ecstatic. For ten years he and Meers had been working on finding the last stone. The first three had been discovered in different parts of the world: Australia, South Africa, and Eastern China. At first, knowledge of the finds had been kept a heavily guarded secret by each of the governments that had discovered them yet, like any news of this magnitude, the information had leaked out and, once the designs had been deciphered and translated, the race for the fourth and final stone had begun. Peters knew it was in Alaska, in the barely explored region of the Triangle, and now he had confirmation. Here it stood in front of him, ready to validate the work he'd staked his career and life on.

Overhead, a bird suddenly darted across the valley, uttering a shrill scream as it went. Everyone looked up and Peters felt his heart flip at the shockingly loud sound of it. He looked around at the others, seeing the same sudden fear on their faces.

"There's our screamer from last night," Meers said, looking up at the sky.

"It didn't really sound like that," one of the students said, her voice wavering and frightened.

"Sound carries differently down here. Come on, let's get this dug out underneath and we can quit for the night."

With an end in sight, the others went back to work in a frenzy of activity and the stone was gently rocked onto its side and carefully set down in the trailer of one of the heavy movers they'd brought. With this final piece, they would be able to decode the mystery of the key to the doorway and be able to open it to see what lay beyond. Peters and Meers were intensely eager to get their find back to their university lab and get to work but he knew he would need to bring in the scientists who had found the other stones. Before that happened, Peters wanted more time with it after searching for so long. He helped tie the stone down and then he and the others picked up the lanterns for the walk back to the trail that led up to the campsite. Taking one more quick look at the stone, he was surprised to see a faint glow coming off where it loomed in the dark, even laid over on its side. He made a mental note to examine it further in the morning and then turned and hurried after the others who had gone ahead of him.

The darkness was nearly complete in the valley and each of the students walked in their own blob of lantern light. Peters quickened his pace, nearly jogging, yet those blobs seemed to be pulling away from him. He broke into a light run but still they got further ahead until he could see the first light begin the winding trek up the trail.

"Hey! Wait a moment!" He called out but his voice fell flat and still the light pulled away until he was on his own in the dark valley. Overhead, the screaming bird flew by again, though this time it sounded lower, closer. Peters ducked down reflexively and lifted the lantern, but the glow was feeble and, even as he watched, it seemed to shrink in closer to him. Panic began to edge at him and he turned and began to jog in earnest, letting out a short cry as the last of the lanterns disappeared up over the lip of the valley. Alone now in a sea of pressing darkness, Peters broke into a run, unmindful of the rock that littered the valley floor. He could see the beginning of the trail and he broke into a sprint only to trip on a sudden jut of rock that sent him sprawling to the ground. He slid a little across the ground and lay panting, the lantern just out of arms reach. As he watched it, trying to catch his breath, the light began to flicker.

Panting now in fear and the pain in his foot and leg, Peters scrambled to his feet and hopped to where the lantern lay, grabbing it and hurrying as fast as his newly injured leg would allow. He took a few more hobbling steps, ready to set his feet on the trail, only to look down in shock as he found himself standing over the portal stone where it lay on its side, tied to the trailer. Blinking in confusion, he turned and could just see the light from the campsites fire, far across the valley floor and up the trail, just where he should be standing now. Heavy flapping overhead made him duck down as something huge passed over, though there was no accompanying cry this time. In the darkness around him, he could hear sudden footfalls that seemed to be running around him. He turned with the sound, clutching the lantern close, even as its light continued to fade. A hushed whispering broke out, the sound of many someone's out in the darkness beyond his circle of light and then more footfalls joined in until it sounded as if dozens of *somethings* were darting around him.

"Come out, come to the light," Peters called out, appalled at the quavering fear in his voice. The sound of his voice made the fear in his stomach ratchet up even further and, when his lantern suddenly, shockingly, went dark, Peters screamed in terror. Behind him, the stone gave off a thin, blue glow and he rushed over, desperate for any source of light. The footsteps began to press in on him, the whispering growing louder as whoever was hiding in the darkness snuck toward him. Peters was panting heavily, his eyes as wide as possible as he frantically searched the darkness. When the first shape, an inky black in the gloom of the valley, moved in his field of vision, he screamed again. It was massive and seemed horribly misshapen as it lurched just out of clear sight. He caught sight of another, and another, until he realized he was surrounded. The whispering started up again though now it was coming from behind him, from within the stone.

You sought the doorway. Now you have found it. Through the doorway, we will take you. Come, rejoice in the beautiful terror that awaits.

Peters screamed again and kept screaming as the shapes lumbered forward and grabbed at him. They scrabbled at his skin with rancid claws, spiked tentacles, and putrid decaying flesh even as they pulled him through the stone.

o

The screams died away as the group stood at the lip of the valley looking down, uneasy at the terror that had been in the sound.

"That's some bird," the guide said in a joking tone that fell flat.

"I'm glad this is our last night out here. This valley gives me the creeps," one of the grad students said, her arm slipping through that of one of the male students who swelled with false bravado as he held her. He didn't think he would have to sleep alone tonight and he silently thanked the scary bird that could sound so much like a terrified man.

"We're *sure* no one is missing?" Meers, the leader of this university expedition, asked as he surveyed the group.

"Everyone is accounted for, I double-checked myself," the guide told him.

"Very well. Let's get some sleep then, I want to be back at the airfield before the week is out once we get that stone up here." Meers didn't wait for the others but went straight to his tent and climbed into his sleeping bag. He stayed awake for nearly an hour thinking about his find, desperately glad that he had been able to locate the stone after so long. No one had expected him, on his own, to discover its location. The key to a doorway that he was eager to open. He fell asleep and dreamed of the awards and journal articles and accolades he would receive for his solo work.

In the morning, the trailer holding the stone was driven carefully out of the valley and, with the campsite packed up, the group headed back the way they had come nearly a month ago. Left behind at the edge of the valley sat a single tent, the opening unzipped, its contents open to the elements. No one had packed it up, no one had even noticed it. As time passed and the weather changed, the tent faded, rotted, collapsed, until it was covered over with grass and time, forgotten.

Deep in the Blue

Coiled and still, the creature slept in the depths of its cavernous home. It had no concept of time and so had no concept of how long it had lain in the cave, dormant and alone. On the surface, eons had passed yet nothing going on above had managed to wake it, not since it had originally found this planet and this cavern.

A cosmic traveler, the creature had spanned incalculable distances in its exploration of space, passing through galaxies and solar systems until it had felt the life-giving pull of a young, blazing star. The creature had gone straight for it, bathing in the hot aura of its rays before detecting the tantalizing scent of water that pulsed out from a planet slightly farther away. Leaving the regenerative cloud of the sun, the creature coiled its way through the vacuum of space until it found the blue planet. It passed easily through the thick atmosphere and sped straight for the deep blue-green vastness of the ocean that spread along the surface, splashing down and letting the water soak through every pore and scale. For years it lay stretched along the bottom, feeling sand and debris and dead things fall down over it until it resembled another underwater mountain formation.

Eventually, sleep began to close in, as it always did, and the creature stirred and rose to the surface, propelling itself into the air as it started its search for a deep place to rest. While it had lay under the waves, filling itself with water and feeling the sun's rays that were nourishment to it, the planet had grown and changed. The creature passed over the minds of massive beasts that lumbered over the earth and rumbled through the oceans. All were a miniscule fraction to its own massive size, yet it was surprised to find such creatures when before, there had been almost nothing. It dismissed the creatures below; they were basic, animalistic, and posed no threat. It traveled nearly the length of the entire planet, finding deep pockets, none of which could offer the refuge that it sought.

Finally, it found a cavern. One that ran deep into the earth and spanned the miles that the creature would need to house its bulk. There was no opening that it could find, no way to reach the cavern, so the creature simply bored through the layers of rock and soil until it reached the opening below. Satiated from milennia of absorbing water and sunlight, the creature relaxed into the chambers of the massive cavern and, slowly, fell into deep sleep.

The sun passed overhead and the moon following, thousands, millions of times while it slept in the earth. Creatures died and were born, new species created and lost. The earth groaned itself apart and back together yet none of that affected the creature or disturbed its long rest. When a section of the cavern collapsed and flooded the system with water, the creature stirred ever so slightly, yet ultimately even that wasn't enough to wake it and so, it slept on.

○

"Hey Barry, can you still hear me down there? I'm getting some interference."

"Yeah, Craig I still read you. You're loud and clear on my end."

"Alright, must be the gear up here. I'm still getting the picture coming through, so that's good news at least. Can you pan over to those stalactites again? Dr. Robison wanted to get a lot of footage and some rock samples if you guys can swing it."

"Yep, got it." Barry Thompson rolled his eyes in the wide, face-covering dive mask he wore and, across from him in the water, Ella Mackey smiled wide. There was plenty of light where they were hovering in Belize's Great Blue Hole and their flashlights illuminated an even larger portion. They wouldn't be going very deep on this dive, just far enough to have drifted down to the stalactite formations that had been created when this cave system was empty of the water that now flooded it. Below, the bottom fell away to darkness and Barry tried not to look down. They all knew what was down there; a toxic layer of hydrogen sulfide that had claimed the lives of possibly thousands of small creatures that had fallen and died in the anoxic environment. The darkness under his lazily paddling flippers was nearly complete and, despite *knowing* what was there, Barry still found himself feeling disoriented and strangely terrified if he looked down there for too long. So, he simply didn't.

He swam closer to the stalactite formations, moving the dive camera slowly over as much of them as he could. Close by, Ella was collecting small bits and storing them in the dive bag she carried at her waist. Moving slightly further into the side cavern that contained most of the formations, Barry was watching the camera screen as he panned it slowly across the darkened area when a heavy shift in the water made him grunt in surprise.

"Barry? You feel that?" Ella asked, her voice heavy with worry and surprise.

"Yeah, maybe a small earthquake?"

"You felt something?" Craig's voice jumped into their ears and Barry nodded before remembering that Craig couldn't see them.

"Yeah, a shift in the water. Anyone registering earthquakes?"

"Not that I can tell. I'll have Sanders check on that. Can you continue?"

Barry didn't answer for several moments and let himself drift to the rock shelf that held the stalactites. He waited, head cocked, to see if the movement would happen again, but there was nothing.

"I think we're good. I have another fifteen minutes of oxygen, so we'll be up soon anyway."

"Alright, keep me posted. And this footage is excellent. Keep it up"

Barry didn't roll his eyes this time, he wanted to film as much as he could before they went back up. Glancing down, Barry thought for a moment that there was more light in the depths and he could see a curious swirling but then Ella was calling him over so he went, ignoring the darkness.

"Barry, look at this." Ella was holding up what looked like a piece of a scale, broken off. She laid it in his hand and he brought it up close to the face mask to get more light on it. It looked like the point of a shark scale, or something similar, yet it was massive in his hand, even with it obviously being broken at some point. He turned it over in the light, marveling at the way it changed color as he moved it, ranging from a deep, purple-black to a bright, fiery orange.

"What is it, do you think?" she asked, watching the play of light over the color changes. Barry shook his head.

"I can't even hazard a guess. Mark might know," he handed the scale back to Ella who stowed it in her dive bag.

"I guess it's a good thing a biologist tagged along this time." Barry nodded, exaggerating the movement so she could see it around all of his gear but he didn't answer. A strange sort of vertigo was eating at him and, unsure why, he looked down again. Barry gasped and kicked up slightly causing Ella to look sharply at him.

"Barry? What? Do we need to go back up?"

"There's something down there!" he cried out in a strangled voice. "I saw something move!"

"What?" Ella moved to the edge of the shelf and looked down. "I don't see anything. There can't be anything down there though Barry, there's no oxygen at the bottom."

"I saw it, it's massive! Let's go, let's get back up." He grabbed the camera and started up but was jerked to a stop by Ella grabbing his arm.

"Okay, we'll go up. But not that fast. Barry, calm down and let's go up slowly, okay?" She held his arms in a tight grip and the pressure calmed him slightly. Barry blew out a shaky breath and nodded.

"Yeah, calm and slow. You're right. Sorry about that, I got spooked."

"No kidding, this place is beyond creepy though. I'm glad this is my last dive down here, if I'm going to be honest." The two of them started their slow ascent, letting Craig know that they were surfacing.

At the surface, Barry pulled the mask from his face and took a deep gulp of air, glad to out of the depths. The research ship was floating near them and the two divers kicked their way over, letting the people in the boat help haul them out of the water. Their dive gear was heavy and Barry was glad of the boost. He sat for a moment on the platform, his flippered feet dangling in the water and that rush of vertigo hit him again, this time accompanied by a surge of terror that left him nearly hyperventilating. Craig shook him by the shoulder.

"Barry? Hey man, what's going on? Here, let's get this gear off you." Craig and Ella hauled Barry into the boat and helped him take off the heavy gear. As soon as the dive hood was off, Barry stood and turned to the other two.

"Let's go, get this boat across the reef, now."

"Barry, what…."

"I'm not fucking around here Craig. Get it moving now, something's wrong. There might have been another collapse down there, something, but we have to go. *Now.*"

"Yeah, alright. I'll tell Phil." Craig moved toward the cabin of the ship and Barry was gratified to see that he was hurrying. He didn't let his shoulders relax, though, until Phil had started the engine and turned the boat toward the opening in the reef. Ella touched his arm and Barry turned to her.

"You alright?"

"No, there's something down there. Maybe not, you know, something alive, but a collapse or shift in the cavern. It feels…off, I don't know." Ella looked back at where they'd come out of the water, now frothed and rippling from where the boat had passed.

"You think that's what that pressure was that we felt?"

"I don't know, maybe. I'll just be glad to be away from here. I have a really bad feeling, and I never get those."

They were just nearing one of the entrances to the formation when the water around them began to shudder. Ella gasped at the sight and clutched at Barry's arm and, behind him, he could hear Craig exclaiming at the sight of the water. It looked like it was boiling and, beyond the circular opening of the Hole, they could see the reef beginning to jitter and jump. A helicopter, someone's leisure craft, blasted by overhead, heading for the center and then hovering fairly low over the water.

"They need to get out of there," Barry said softly, faintly.

"What the hell is this?" Craig shouted, his voice carrying over the water though there was a massive rumbling just starting to fill the air. It quickly eclipsed the thumping blades of the helicopter and, as everyone on the boat watched in horrified fascination, the water pushed upward as something drove skyward from beneath the waves. They watched as the helicopter tried to bank away but it was too slow and the rushing gout of water smashed into it, causing a small, fiery explosion that they could feel even in the boat. In the pilot house, their ship captain pushed the throttle forward, throwing them slightly off balance as he forced the boat to go as possible.

"That is not a geyser," Ella said and, as they watched, the water began to fall away, exposing the head and neck of a monster.

"What in the actual hell..." Craig breathed out.

Beside him, Ella was making a strange sound and, when he turned to her, Barry choked out a gasping scream. She had been staring at the creature that was even yet still rising from the Hole but now she was spasming, her whole body jerking roughly as she stood in the boat. Blood and smoking gore was streaming from her eyes and mouth and she was emitting harsh clicking sounds that sounded like nothing a human should be able to make. Craig smacked him and Barry turned, eyes wide and terrified to see the same thing happening to the large man. Barry backed away from them, his eyes glancing at the creature before he turned and fled toward the front of the boat. The engines were straining as they fought against the pull of water back to where they'd been. To where the monster, the massive and unbelievable *thing* was blotting out most of the sky. He could feel now a deep thrum in his bones, a horrible grinding sound that seemed to eat at him from the inside and Barry could hear himself panting in panicked fear. He looked in the pilot house and met the eyes of Phil who was hunched over the steering wheel, his fingers in a vise grip around it. Phil looked as terrified as Barry felt but he didn't stop, he wanted to get as far from the creature as he could.

The backward pull on the boat suddenly stopped and then seemed to reverse as a massive wave pushed out toward them, hurtling the boat forward. Barry clutched at the rail, refusing to look behind them. They passed a yacht and all over the decks, scantily clad men and women were either shrieking in fear or were in the midst of the same seizures that affected Ella and Craig. They passed close enough that Barry could see the smoking holes where their eyes had been. He swallowed hard, squeezed his eyes shut and, for the first time in his life, Barry prayed fervently and hard for God to save him.

When the boat engines wound down, the sound jarred Barry back to himself and he opened his eyes, aghast that the boat was slowing to a stop. He whirled around, only to see Phil leaving the cabin and going towards the boats stern.

"No, no no!" He shouted. "Phil! Get back in there!" Phil didn't answer and Barry knew that if he rounded the pilot house, he would see Phil jittering and jerking. The sky was dark now but Barry stubbornly kept his eyes on everything except the horizon behind him. He turned and lifted his leg over the side when something vast and incomprehensible brushed against his mind. It felt to Barry like a snake tongue licking at his brain. He shrieked and dropped to the bottom of the boat, his hands clutching at his head. When he rolled to his back and looked up, the creature was there but creature was not the right word. There was no word of Man that could describe what stared down at him, its mind burrowing into his own with careful, surgical precision. He felt it rummage around in his brain and felt the moment that it dismissed him before his brain exploded inside his skull and Barry died silently with his mouth open.

o

Awakened and aware, the monster uncoiled from its cavernous home, its body filling the world around it for hundreds of miles. It could sense the minds that littered the planet, feeling them as they winked out all around it. They were little more than the animalistic minds that it had sensed so long ago, when it first found this place yet there were more, far, far more than it had felt before. They died easily enough, moving on to the next plane where they might, eventually, grow into something more complex. The monster itself had, after all, been something as simple as these minute and dismissible beings once. Fully on the surface, the monster could feel the panic of the tiny beings as it spread around the globe, creating a massive shriek that jangled at its own mind. The sheer volume of them all screaming at once was too much for one who had had peace for so long. It stretched its body up through the clouds, unfurling delicate, membranous wings and blared its voice across the world, careful to target only those creatures that had been the cause of the moment of pain. In an instant they were snuffed out as one, the great mass of them moving on from this plane in a sighing exodus of silence.

The creature sifted through what remained, surprised to find a few of the beings still clinging to life and decided to leave them and this planet. A planet that was far too occupied in any case and would die before the monster. Already it could feel the rot at the surface. It pushed itself into the sky, wings pumping easily until it broke through into the humming stillness of the great darkness. Angling for the sun for a last rejuvenating blast, the monster moved on to find another world, another place to rest as it slowly explored universe after universe. Though it had lived for countless millennia, there was still so much to see.

○

Rebecca stepped out of her apartment and looked up at the sky with a horror-filled, tear-stained face. She could feel liquid running from her ears and when she touched them, her fingers came away red. She snapped her fingers twice, three times, and sobbed aloud, though now she could not hear it, as she realized that whatever had made that hideous sound, had deafened her. Behind her, in the house, her parents and two younger brothers lay dead in a terrifying rictus of crooked limbs and smoking, blood-filled eye sockets. She had watched as they died in agony, their shrieks falling on her newly deafened ears.

She walked down the street, her head swiveling from house to house, to all of the cars, parked and crashed, hoping to find someone else. *Anyone* else who had survived whatever it was that had happened. There had been mere moments it seemed, less than ten full minutes of news coverage of *something* coming out of the sea and then everyone had died. She sobbed again, the sound falling on a world nearly empty of human life and kept walking down the street.

Around her in the trees, birds sang sweetly, their songs sounding clearer and much louder in the sudden silence of the world.

Survivor One

The end of the world happened slowly enough at first that no one noticed but then suddenly it was over and nearly everyone was dead. It was disease, or chemical warfare, or natural selection. The survivor didn't know; all he knew was that everyone was gone, and it was *exceedingly* inconvenient.

He met Survivors 3 and 4, Joe and Cecily, they called themselves, on week seventeen. When they asked his name, he told them 'Survivor 1'. They weren't sure if he was joking and didn't press but there was some awkward laughter on their part. They didn't ask again.

The end of the world wasn't so bad, Joe and Cecily decided, although it was a lot of work. It would have been better if Survivor 1 would just stop complaining. He complained about *everything*.

"I wish it wasn't so hot."

"Why does it have to be so cold?"

"They could have used solar cells, so we could still have the internet..."

"Why is all this food bad? It hasn't even *been* that long."

"There are too many animals."

"There aren't enough animals! How are we supposed to eat?"

And so on.

Joe and Cecily were tired of it. They had been hoping to find more people (Cecily especially; Joe was nice, but he had too much last-man-on-earth mentality) but after six months, both began trying to find reasons to set out into the wide, empty world.

The reason they stayed so long, and continued to stay, is that Survivor 1 did most of the work and he was *very* good at surviving. He had a small-ish pack which seemed to have the same properties as Merlin's magic bag as he could pull a nearly endless supply of gear from it. Once, Cecily wrote down everything she could see him take out if. Those included:

(1) Small hatchet with cover

(6) packs of matches in a small, watertight case

(2) packs of regular Skittles

(2) small spools of fishing line

(7) fishhooks stabbed into a cork

(1) brown notebook

(1) pack of pens

(2) ponchos rolled into tiny balls

(1) small pistol

(6) cases of bullets for the pistol

(4) cases of bullets for a rifle he carried over the pack

(1) folding stool (how???)

(2) long knives

(1) small, floppy-eared stuffed bunny

After the bunny, she stopped watching.

Survivor 1 made their fires, set up campsites, went in to houses first with his rifle drawn and ready, hunted and dressed the kills, cooked, cleaned up, treated injuries, kept watch and any other of the thousand things they had to do to survive. That was why, six months after meeting him, Joe and Cecily were only now thinking more seriously of leaving.

He made the end of the world easy but his bitter, unceasing complaints were more than anyone could handle.

On the day they decided to leave, Survivor 1 already knew, and he gave them one of his knives to take. On this day he did not complain, and Cecily couldn't take it.

"Why?" she cried out. "Why is it that you complain so much when the world as we know it has ended?"

"Because," he replied mildly. "I didn't expect to be one of the survivors."

Exasperated with his answer, Joe and Cecily left. They headed south as winter was approaching and a Georgia winter sounded better than a Michigan one. Survivor 1 watched them leave and then packed his small bag and headed for one of the many lakes that were packed with cabins. The last cabin he'd stayed at with 3 and 4 had been a pre-fab, which he hadn't realized, and it wouldn't last much longer. Survivor 1 planned on finding a sturdy, well-maintained cabin where he could begin to settle in. The end of the world was so much work and he sighed heavily thinking about everything he'd have to do in order to prepare for the second winter after the end.

He walked for three days and on the fourth, he found a dog. It wagged its tail at him, though it was skinny and sad, and snapped the meat out of the air that he threw at it. When he patted his thigh, the dog followed him, so he named it Survivor 5 and together they walked the miles to the lake.

The dog made the days and long nights more bearable as it was friendly with its affection and helped him flush game. When they reached the lake, it passed several cabins before climbing the steps of an older, neatly dressed cabin and lying down on the porch with a heavy sigh. Survivor 1 looked at no others and, that day, began to settle them in. He chopped wood, raided the other cabins, found a bike with an attached carrier that he could use to haul food and supplies, cleaned the cabin and fitted it up with everything he thought he would need, including four boxes of books tucked away in one of the attics.

When the leaves were ankle deep on the ground, Survivors 1 and 5 surveyed the cabin with pride and then turned to see a small girl standing at the end of the driveway. She was skittish, wide-eyed and dirty, and not much older than ten. Survivor 1 couldn't imagine how she'd spent the last two years on her own and survived. 5 walked toward her, tongue lolling and tail wagging slowly and, when he reached her, he dropped to the ground, rolled on his back, and presented his stomach for a scratch. The girl darted at look at 1, who didn't move, before reaching down and giving 5 a quick pet. When 5 stood, he shook himself, licked her hand, and walked back up the driveway, stopping at 1 to look back at the girl. 1 looked at 5 and then at the girl and sighed.

"I've food inside and there's an extra room with a nice bed. If you want, I can start the generator so you can take a bath. The door is unlocked." He and 5 went inside but it was twenty minutes before the girl ghosted her way through the door, barely making a sound. 1 pointed to the table where he'd set out food for her and then went back to reading in front of the fire. She ate quickly but quietly and cleared her spot. When she tiptoed into the living room, 1 stood up and beckoned her to follow. He started the tub, laid out a towel, and then set a basket full of girls clothes he'd found in the house right inside the door so she could change. Then he went back to his book. 5 sighed in his sleep in front of the fire.

The girl bathed and changed and cleaned up after herself and 1 realized he hadn't complained even once. When the girl came out, she saw 5 on the floor and curled up with him in front of the fire. When 1 got tired an hour later, he set his book down, then carried the girl to one of the spare rooms, tucked her in then went to his own bed. He lay awake for a time, thinking of how much else he'd have to set aside to feed one more mouth and then wondered what her name might be. After long moments, he got up and pulled the stuffed bunny from the pack he'd stored in his closet. It had belonged to his daughter who had been one of the first to die. He used to call her Tooty-Fruity as a joke, Two for short, a joke she'd loved. He had no more tears for his long dead daughter, his grief had nearly killed him at the time, and so, when he looked at the bunny he could feel the sadness of missing her but, behind it was the life he still had stretching before him.

He pressed the bunny to his nose and inhaled deeply before getting up and going to the girl's room. He tucked the bunny next to her on the pillow and when she turned in her sleep and cuddled it close, Survivor 1 sighed and spoke softly.

"My name is Paul."

Then he left, 5's tail thumping softly on the girl's bed where he lay and Paul thought about all the work left to do to prepare three survivors for winter. For once since the end, he looked forward to it.

Teddy Bear

Headlights swept through the twilight darkened house, glimmering over dusty, bare floors, empty rooms, and a cavernous and empty fireplace before coming to a rest on one previously shadowed corner which held a small, ragged teddy bear. The light abruptly cut off with the cease of the car engine outside and the sound of four doors slamming reverberated through the empty rooms of the big house.

Outside, Robert Faine surveyed the house with immense satisfaction. His wife, Charlotte, took his arm, her cheek resting on his shoulder as she looked up with him, admiring the Gothic architecture, even in such a rundown state. Behind them, their three children looked on in disbelief at the decrepit air of the place.

"This is gross," the eldest, Ella, said with disgust on her face. "We have to sleep here tonight? We don't even have beds."

"No sweetie, we'll be at the motel tonight since the movers won't be here until tomorrow. I just wanted us to come and take a look around," Robert told his daughter, stepping back to his children and wrapping an arm around her shoulders.

"We don't have flashlights dad," Levi said and his brother Adam, identical in looks but not personality nodded.

"Yeah, is there even electricity?"

"There should be, why don't we go find out?" Robert took his arm from Ella's shoulder and grabbed his wife's hand so that the two of them could lead the way into the house, their three children straggling in behind. Once inside, Robert dropped his wife's hand to use his phone flashlight to search for the light switch. It took him several moments to locate it and by then, everyone was inside. They could hear him grumbling as he ran his light over the wall and then a loud, "aha!" and the room brightened slightly, a faint buzz accompanying the electricity.

"It's still dark, dad," Ella said, crossing her arms against a heavy uneasiness she began to feel as she looked around the shadowed room.

"Give it a minute, the lighting is old so it takes a while for the bulbs to warm up." Sure enough, the room began to lighten perceptibly until they were all standing in the well-lit entryway. Ahead, the house opened up into a massive living room space with a fireplace that dominated nearly the whole back wall. To their right, was a staircase to the second floor and a door that led into what looked like a kitchen. Robert strode into the big open space of the living room and put his fists on his hips, posing like a conquering warrior. He looked back at them, a smile plastered on his face and Charlotte, clapping like a schoolgirl, skipped to join him. They wrapped their arms around each other and surveyed the space. Ella, standing behind them, felt the uneasiness that had gripped her pulse wildly and she swallowed around a hot lump of fear. Confusion at the emotion made her look around to find what could be causing it, but the house was empty except for them. On this level anyway.

Levi and Adam stepped into the room and began the serious business of exploring. Now that the lights were on and flooding each corner, the scary atmosphere had left for them and they were excited for a massive space to investigate. Ella, rubbing her arms, moved closer to the fireplace. She could imagine a roaring fire in the empty space and wished there was one now, the chill of the room was getting to her.

As she got closer, she noticed a small, lumpen shape tucked against the brick work, in a corner where it met the wall. Her first thought was that there was a rat but when it didn't move, she stepped closer, leaning over for a better look. The shape resolved itself into a worn and very old teddy bear, much of its padding gone. The eyes were, strangely, devoid of any of the dust that coated the fireplace and floor and, without thinking, Ella picked it up.

The room disappeared; her parents, brothers, everything, and Ella was standing in a rotting pit filled with heaps of corpses. She tore her eyes from the bear and looked around, her breath beginning to come in heaving, choked gasps as she struggled to comprehend what had just happened. Under her feet, the jumbles of corpses began to roil and pitch. Ella tried to open her hand to drop the bear but thick, yellow spikes shot out from the bear's stuffed body and latched onto her hand, spilling blood all over her shoes. Ella looked down, sucked in a breath, and shrieked in the bear's face. It turned then, and blinked its eyes which shifted from black buttons to pits filled with fire.

Ahhhhhhh, a voice sighed in the air around her, drowning out her pain and terror-filled shrieks. *A lovely soul, uncharacteristically free from avarice and greed, pure and delicious. Come, sweet child, and let me devour you.*

As the bear swelled in her hands, its spikes growing larger and thicker and piercing up into her arms, Ella's shrieks became wails of gibbering horror. Hands on her arms pulled her back unexpectedly and, wails trailing off, Ella blinked and was back in the living room, her brothers staring at her with wide, frightened eyes.

"Ella, why are you screaming?" Levi asked, his hands gripping her tight on the arm. Ella looked down at the bear which had a yarn smile that she could have sworn wasn't there before and she threw it, hard, into the fireplace, once more wishing for a blazing fire in the center.

"We have to go," she croaked out, her voice hoarse and rough. "Where's mom and dad?"

"They went upstairs," Adam told her, his hand creeping into hers while his eyes remained fixed on the bear.

"Ella, you didn't say why you were screaming though," Levi said again, his voice rising into panic.

"I'll tell you in the car, now come *on*. We have to get mom and dad and get out of here." She took them both by the hand and rushed toward the stairs, taking them two at a time even as her brothers stumbled up behind her. Neither said a word but she could hear the rising fear in their labored breaths.

"Mom?" she called out, going to the first room. It was empty so she hurried down to the next. "Mom, dad, where are you guys?" Each room was empty and Ella broke out in a sweat as her skin prickled with adrenaline and fear.

"What's that door?" Adam asked and when she looked down at him, he was pointing down a side hallway where an open doorway sat in heavy shadow.

"Goddamnit," Ella whispered, her stomach clenching but she pulled her brothers with her toward the door. Just inside the doorway, stairs led up into darkness and Ella would have backed away except that she could hear footsteps up there.

"Mom?" Adam called out suddenly, making Ella jump and clamp down on their hands. "Sorry," he said sheepishly. She just shook her head at him and gave him a quick smile.

"Mom, dad? You up there?" Ella called out into the dark. Heavy whispering floated down to them and all three backed away until a voice followed.

"Up here, darlings. We're just taking a peek at the attic," their mother's voice spiraled down to them but it was off, not her usual voice.

"Mom, we want to go. Can you guys come down?"

"Of course, daaarlings. Why don't you come up and look around first? This will make an exsssssssellent playroom for the boys."

Adam started to walk forward but Ella pulled him back, her brow furrowing. When she stepped backward, taking them both with her, the whispering started up again.

"Ella, she said to go up," Levi said, his face heavy with worry.

"We're not, no way. Come on, let's get out of here now," she turned and both boys followed her even though she had let go of their hands. Rushing back out to the main hallway, Ella turned toward the stairs going back down only to skid to a stop at a massive shadow lurching upward toward them.

"The bear," Adam said, his voice shaking. Ella looked down at him. "Ella, that's the bear!" He was backing away from her and the shape shoving its way up the stairs but, just as he backed to the hallway, a hand snaked out and clutched him around the neck.

"Adam!" She and Levi screamed his name at the same time and Levi rushed forward, Ella's hands slipping off his shirt as she tried to grab him.

"Levi, no!" she shrieked but now her parents were looming out from around the corner and Ella fell back a step involuntarily at the sight of them. They were grotesque, their bodies melded together at the waist, the flesh like cooled wax. Where their arms had been, there was now a single writhing appendage with hooked spikes running the length and, as he ran up to his brother in a panic of terror, that appendage lashed out and took Levi's head off, snatching it before it could hit the ground. Ella screamed and Adam's eyes bulged though his gaping mouth made no sound.

Levi's body slumped to the ground just as what had been their parents came fully into the hallway. Not-Charlotte turned to smile at Ella, her bottom jaw dropping open in a parody of a smile but then it kept going until the entire front of her torso was a gaping mouth full of rows and rows of teeth. It turned back to Adam and, before Ella could comprehend it, Not-Charlotte snapped forward and bit through his midsection, ripping him open to the spine. Adam's eyes rolled back and his arms dropped limply to his side as he died and Ella, now breathing in hitching, gasping breaths, backed away from the monster that had killed her parents and brothers.

"*Ssssssssweeeeeetieee, dooon't go faaaar. Your mmmmmotherrr and I nnnneeeeeed to ssssssssspeak to youuu.*" The half that had been her father stretched up around the Not-Charlotte, his neck lengthening and coiling like a mutated snake. The creature dropped Adam's body to fall in a crumpled heap on top of Levi's before it turned and took a lurching step forward. Ella could feel her mind slipping, the scene before her was simply too much to take in. Her fingers had dug into her cheeks as she backed away, her eyes wide and fixed and, when she thumped into something soft and yielding, she knew her life was over. Craning her neck around, Ella locked eyes with the bear that was grown into a massive, humped monster. Legs were sprouting from its side, even as she watched and when the first spikes shot from its stomach and pierced her from the back of her head down her body, Ella couldn't make a sound. Mouth gaping, she made a harsh, choking sound as the spikes lengthened and punched through the other side of her body. She swiveled her eyes to see the thing that had been her parents crawling forward to lick the blood that was flowing freely from the hundreds of wounds that covered her. Her death was slow and, as she felt her mind and life going, Ella felt the Not-Charlotte pulling itself up her body until it was face to face with her, tongue lapping over her eyes where tears mingled with blood. It smiled and Ella died with a scream stuck in her throat.

In the house, the floorboards rippled, becoming the surface of a pond that pulled the corpses into its depths. The Not-Parents, now fully transformed, slipped into the pool after them, eager to explore the noxious and inhuman plane that had reached across the cosmos to birth it. The bear, back to its normal, teddy size and back in its place, slumped once more in the corner of the living room. Behind its eyes, the sweet souls of the children it had consumed shrieked in agony within the universe it held inside itself.

Outside, a snakelike appendage slid from the deep woods, wrapped itself around the car, and drug it back into the trees. Again the house would wait for the next to feel its pull. Until then, all would slumber.

Area 51

Dr. Childs read through the one-page document that had been carried into his office by three heavily armed guards and who now waited patiently as he finished it and read it again. Finally, after clearing his throat, Dr. Childs looked up and raised his eyebrows.

"When you're ready, sir, we'll take you to the airfield," one of the men said, the many bars on his collar insignia suggesting he was in charge.

"Uh, I'm not sure I want to get involved in this."

"Too late for that sir, you've read the document. Your apartment was already packed up and your affairs put in order here. When you're ready."

Dr. Childs swallowed down the outrage and sudden fear that coated his throat. He knew he shouldn't have accepted the envelope, shouldn't have signed the iPad they put in front of him, shouldn't even have let them into his office. He stood, pushed his chair in and looked around his office. Misinterpreting the look, the soldier spoke up.

"This will all be sent to you in your new office, sir."

"Great," Dr. Childs said, and swallowed again before following the three men out. His colleagues in the office were watching intently, confusion evident on all of their faces. Dr. Childs put a reassuring smile on his face and nodded his way out of the building to the military vehicle that waited outside.

Six hours later, he was in the back of a very comfortable van rolling through the desert and looking out at nothing. He glanced over the first page of the much more substantial packet he'd been handed on the plane to get to this desert, excitement and anxiety warring within him at what waited ahead. The van slowed and he looked through the windshield at the fence and gatehouse ahead. A lone guard came out of the gatehouse, hands ready on his weapon, but the driver gave him the proper credentials and they were waved through the gate.

Another two hours and four additional gates later, and the van was crunching over the lip of an underground parking garage. Despite the blasting A/C, the relief of the van escaping the heavy southern sun was immediate and Dr. Childs shivered in the sudden chill that he was sure wasn't all due to the darkness of the garage. The drive was shorter than he'd thought and, as they parked, two smiling men greeted Dr. Childs as he hopped out of the van.

"Dr. Childs, we're so pleased that you're finally here! I'm Dr. Harris and this is Dr. Forlaine. I can get that bag for you," he took Dr. Childs' bag without waiting for an okay and Dr. Childs just let him, slightly overwhelmed by the younger man's bright enthusiasm.

"We'll show you to your rooms and then your office," Dr. Forlaine said, his soft voice and gentle demeanor a balm compared to the harsh landscape and Dr. Harris's overt brightness. Dr. Childs followed them up a short flight of stairs and then down one of the longest hallways he'd ever seen. Room after room, doors all shut, but with massive, floor-to-ceiling windows lined the hallway and Dr. Childs couldn't resist swiveling his head to look through each one. Most were boring, mundane rooms filled with filing cabinets or cubical offices, hunch-backed workers typing away at monotonous screens filled with numbers and data. Other rooms were more interesting, full of lab equipment or rows of cages filled with animals that he couldn't identify due to the fast pace the other two men and their military escort took. He assumed they were rats.

Finally, the hallway curved gently to the right and they came to a set of double doors that looked like blast doors from a sci-fi movie. Dr. Harris and Dr. Forlaine stepped up to a double panel in the righthand door and Dr. Childs waited while they went through an elaborate system of checking eyes and full handprints and then a lengthy password. The doors slowly opened and Dr. Forlaine turned with a somewhat embarrassed smile.

"You'll get set up tomorrow for security. The government, you know," he gave a small shrug and turned to follow Dr. Harris. Dr. Childs followed them both, the guard escort at his back.

Confusingly, the massive doors opened into what looked like a hotel lobby. There was a comfortable lounge area, a fully stocked bar behind a set of decorated glass doors and, ahead, a front desk counter, complete with a smiling hostess.

"Welcome Dr. Childs," the woman told him, her voice low and melodious. "If you'll step to the counter, I'll get you checked in." Dr. Childs looked to the other two doctors who merely smiled blandly at him and, feeling slightly uncomfortable, he did what she asked, resting one hand on the counter. After typing for a few short moments on a keyboard, the woman looked up at him, still smiling, and slid a keycard and a name badge onto the counter. He stretched his hand forward to reach them when a beep sounded and a panel under his hand opened up. Dr. Childs snatched his hand back but the women wasn't phased.

"For formal identification and full access to the facility, please place your hand on the scanner." Dr. Childs looked at her and at the panel before slowly resting his hand down. A searing pain rippled through his hand, all the way to his bones, but it was so fast he had only time for a short, stunned gasp before the pain and the scanner were gone, tucked back into the desk once more. "Thank you, Dr. Childs, you now have full access to the facility. We have a restaurant staffed at all hours, a gym and Olympic sized swimming pool, should you choose to use them. Additionally, your room and lab are fully staffed with a butler and wait staff for any needs you might encounter while you remain with us. I'll have a porter take your bag and show you to your room."

"Not necessary today Margaret, Dr. Fontaine and I can bring him down."

"Very good Dr. Harris. Enjoy your stay, Dr. Childs. We're all so pleased you're here." Dr. Childs could only nod at her and, now that her speech was over, he noticed that she was oddly still. He turned to follow the other doctors when they prodded him and, when he glanced back, Margaret hadn't moved, smile still pulling her face tight. Unsettled and fully aware that he had likely made a grave mistake in reading that first letter, Dr. Childs followed where he was led.

"Where are the guards?" he asked suddenly, as he and the other two stepped into an elevator.

"Oh, once you speak to Margaret, they are no longer needed so they head back to their station," Dr. Fontaine told him.

"Ah," Dr. Childs said, knowing the inadequacy of the response.

"We have quite a lot of freedom here," Dr. Harris told him. "Despite all the theatrics, this place has been refitted and modernized and we have all the equipment any scientist could ever dream of. If I'd had even a fraction of what they have in the labs downstairs, I'd have never left U of V."

"Did you read the full packet yet?" Dr. Fontaine interrupted. "I know it doesn't give much more than the bare bones, but do you have an idea of where we are on the project here?"

"I admit I was a bit too anxious to read it fully though I did browse through a few pages. I was confused with some of the wording, however, as I'd always thought this facility was meant to study alien life."

"We do, it's just that alien life turned out to be unlike anything anybody had ever expected," Dr. Fontaine replied, his eyes lighting up in an oddly manic way.

"Do you want to get settled in your room first, or head down to the research center?" Dr. Harris asked.

"I can drop my things in my room, if you lead the way. I am more curious than I appear and am looking forward to seeing what it is that I'll be doing here."

"I think we all would be grateful to get things started. We've been stuck in a kind of rut lately which is partly why you've been brought on. Your work has been groundbreaking, and the thought consensus is that by applying your work here, it will revitalize the project," Dr. Forlaine's short speech was impassioned and Dr. Childs wondered which was his real persona; the stoic, calm one or this passionate, almost zealous side. Dr. Childs put his stuff in the living area of his room, taking a moment to glance around at the large space before following the other two to the lab section.

As in the lobby, gone was the sterile, whitewashed façade of the beginning of the facility. Mahogany and wallpapered walls were lit by mellow lighting and, though there was no elevator music piping through well-placed speakers, Dr. Childs didn't have a hard time imagining that he could hear it. Another set of blast door prompted his two escorts to once again repeat the procedure of palms and eyeballs to get them open but, when they did, the doors slid open noiselessly, as though running on silk and that, for a reason he couldn't name, unsettled Dr. Childs even more than the unnerving stillness of the lobby receptionist. It didn't seem that it could be possible for such massive doors to open with the ease of parting a curtain. After a glance to the left and right as he went through, Dr. Childs dismissed the doors as he surveyed the massive room they had just entered, his mind immediately going blank with excitement and awe.

Though the room itself was massive, more a warehouse than a lab, it was divided into multiple sections with thick panes of glass that stretched to the second floor above. He could see dozens of people working diligently in the rooms closest to the door running experiments, collecting data, working computer programs; there was too much to see at once. And then he was again following his escorts as they worked their way through the space.

"The lanes through the sections are marked with black, as you can see here," Dr. Harris said, pointing at lines on the floor as well as arrows on the glass pointing the way.

"Each room is designated with a color scheme as you can see on the doorways. There are a lot of colors but the pattern is easy to learn and is based on the science involved in each room. You'll pick it up in no time."

"And here is our section and where you'll be joining us though you do have your own lab section within," Dr. Harris told him proudly, bringing him to a wall at the back of the room which stretched across the entirety of the back of the space. Dr. Childs noticed that this section had no windows and he wondered at the lack of transparency so prevalent in the rest of this part of the facility.

This door took only one fingerprint and the door opened to reveal a room which reminded Dr. Childs of airlocks he'd seen in science fiction movies. He followed the other doctors through and they waited while the door hissed shut behind them. For several long moments after the door shut, they simply waited, Dr. Childs becoming increasingly impatient at the delay. When his ears popped suddenly, he realized that the room was being pressurized. He looked at Dr. Forlaine who looked at Dr. Harris and then spoke.

"The briefing that was sent was necessarily bare on the details. This facility already has a nefarious reputation, secrets kept and all that, and there are always people trying to get in, both physically and through our networks. The truth, in actuality, is so far different from what people suspect, that the world governments involved in this have deemed it too unsafe for public knowledge. The work that we're doing here goes beyond our lifetime, beyond the lifetime of our children's children, even, and so it will be kept secret for generations to come. On pain of death, which you were told of before you read even that first letter." Dr. Childs nodded reluctantly at Dr. Forlaine's pointed glance and, despite the trepidation and extreme uneasiness that settled in him during this speech, he was eager, more eager than he would have admitted to anyone, to see what lie behind the door. His ears popped again and Dr. Harris spoke.

"Are you ready?"

Dr. Childs nodded and then cleared his throat. "Yes, I'm ready." His ears popped once more, painfully, and then Dr. Forlaine turned to the door, put his hand out, and let it stretch and distend, the fingers elongating and fusing together until what had been a human hand was now the writhing appendage of a monster. Dr. Childs sucked in a breath but remained silent and he let the breath out slowly as Dr. Forlaine's mutated hand and arm plucked faster than he could see at a strangely configured keyboard. Moments later, the door swished open silently and Dr. Childs was staring, eyes wide and fixed, at the room beyond.

"You were chosen because of your work in genetics," Dr. Harris said, his voice now fluting and oddly high. When Dr. Childs turned to look at him, he was not surprised to see a change here as well. Dr. Harris who, moments earlier, had been a short man with a slight belly paunch and a dreadful comb-over, was now nearly two feet taller, thin beyond belief and possessed of elaborately beautiful horns and scales that reflected the light in a prismatic wonder of color. His eyes were slit like a snake, or a dragon, and when a tail swished into view, Dr. Childs had almost suspected it. Dr. Forlaine, when he turned to look at him, had become a creature that looked like a flying or floating octopus though he was more than that. A rigid shell ran over the bulge of his head and he had three pairs of eyes which blinked in tandem. When he spoke, Dr. Childs felt it as a whisper in his mind.

"You have already begun the work of changing your own DNA using the limited technology available on Earth. With the technology this project has found and acquired, the work can be completed. That is also why you were chosen." As the whisper faded, Dr. Forlaine glided into the room and Dr. Childs followed, Dr. Harris stalking behind them. Dr. Forlaine continued speaking as they moved into the room which was dark at this point, everything in shadow.

"Area 51 *was* created because of aliens but the spaceship and bodies in the desert were a distraction, just enough truth to keep people satisfied enough to let it be. The reality is far more out of the realm of expected belief." They reached a point in the dark space and Dr. Forlain stopped. They waited a beat and then lights began to brighten in the room, illuminating what looked like computer workstations centered around a massive and pulsing shape that made odd, trilling noises every few seconds.

"What is that?" Dr. Childs said into the relative quiet of the huge room.

"This is the alien that created the need for Area 51. It is from humanity's future and came here through a wormhole portal, dropped right into the desert. It has been here since then and we learn new things nearly every day."

"What is the project, then? What are you trying to accomplish here? You said the work was stalled but based on your appearances, I find that rather hard to believe."

"Our appearances are surface level, at best. Though we have managed to access genetic and evolutionary data that no one else on Earth has access to, it does not go far enough in our cellular makeup for the end result we are working toward."

"What end result is that?"

Dr. Forlaine did a slow swivel in the air and looked at Dr. Harris who stepped forward.

"Our world is destined to end, we all know that. What was unknown before this creature appeared, is that the end is not billions and billions of years from now. It is a mere thousand years from now. Or, a thousand years from when this alien landed in the desert outside. One thousand years is nothing, a blink of time in the blink of time that humans have existed. What we and the project are trying to do is give humanity a chance outside of the confines of Earth when it does meet its end. This creature has been the key to unlocking that potential. We have already gotten this far," he gestured at his draconian body. "What we need to happen is for these altered bodies to be able to survive in the harshness of space. To do that, we have to unlock the cellular secrets that have, unfortunately, eluded us thus far."

"How do you think that I can make that leap?" Dr. Childs had moved closer to the alien creature, his fascination overcoming any trepidation.

"You used CRISPR technology to alter your own genetic information, something that hasn't been possible outside of developing embryos and petri dishes. We know what you have on your back, and we know that you have managed to keep this breakthrough a secret from the larger community. What we need is to make the connection we have with these genetic changes and connect them to being able to survive outside of our atmosphere. We believe that your research has the answer that we've been searching for."

"And you do the research here, in this room?"

"No, the bulk of the work is done in the room we came through. Here is where we communicate with the creature. It speaks in a series of wavelengths that we convert here through these stations. They convert into human speech through the main station there, all you need to do is put on the headphones."

"That seems a little mundane for the state-of-the-art facility here," Dr. Childs said, even as he stepped forward and put the headphones on. There was a deep hum that filled his teeth with sound before it leveled out and a low growl resolved itself into a single word.

YES?

The voice had a British accent which Dr. Childs found unreasonably hilarious though he managed to keep the laughter down. The next words through the headphones cut the smile from his face and he looked sharply at the creature.

IT IS A PLANET WIDE COLLECTIVE, DR. CHILDS, THAT ANYTHING OUTSIDE THE REALM OF YOUR EXPECATIONS WILL SPEAK WITH A BRITISH ACCENT. I, THEREFORE, SPEAK AS SUCH. YOU ARE HERE, FINALLY, AS I'VE BEEN PROMISED AND NOW THE WORK CAN BEGIN. IF YOU PLEASE, REMOVE THE INFERIORS FROM THE ROOM THAT WE MAY CONVERSE ON THE SAVING OF YOUR SPECIES.

Dr. Childs took the headphones and stepped back, his face white with confused surprise. He turned to doctors Harris and Forlaine who were eagerly watching him. Dr. Childs was even more surprised to find that he could decipher human emotions on the face of such un-humanlike creatures, no matter their base forms.

"He—wants you to go out. He says we have things to discuss and wants us to be alone for it."

"It was the same for each of us, we will go. You may record your conversation with the controls on the left side though sometimes the creature does not wish it. If there is no recording, we have staff who will take down what you can recall and compile a report from that. Should you need anything, simply press the 'Help' button on the console and we will send someone. Enjoy your conversation, it is always very enlightening." With that, both doctors left Dr. Childs who fiddled with the headset once the doors had shut before finally turning back to the creature and slowly putting them back on.

YOUR OUTWARD RELUCTANCE IS AMUSING YET TEDIOUS. YOU HAVE UNLOCKED WHAT THESE INFERIORS COULD NOT AND SO TO YOU I WILL GRANT THE 'SECRET' THAT THEY COULD NOT SEE, EVEN WHEN PRESENTED WITH IT TO THEIR FACES. FIRST, I WOULD SEE YOUR WINGS.

The creature shifted, its bulk seeming to ripple and then a single eye opened in the middle of the gelatinous roundness. It blinked at him, its eye the rectangle that he'd seen in a goat's eye once, and Dr. Childs was held by the gaze for a moment, entranced. It blinked again, breaking the hold on him and he pulled off his suit jacket and dress shirt and turned, letting the wings he'd grown on himself unfurl and spread. They were beautiful and he was intensely vain and proud of them, even if no one else had seen them or knew what he'd done. The work had been simple, almost comically so, and he would have published but something kept him from submitting his final paperwork. And then the envelope had come and it didn't matter anymore. The creature behind him made a gentle, rumbling sigh and Dr. Childs turned back around, letting his wings continue to unfurl and unfold until they arched over his head, the onyx feathers at the bottom gently brushing the concrete of the floor.

SIMPLE, AS YOU SAY, AND YET NO ONE FOUND THE WAY AS YOU DID. NOT ALL WILL AGREE AND HARDLY ANY WILL FOLLOW YOU. YOUR LIFE, FROM HERE, WILL BE DIFFICULT AND UNREWARDING,

UNTIL YOU ATTAIN THE ENLIGHTENMENT THAT AWAITS YOU. AND THEN, ETERNITY IN THE ENDLESS PLANES THAT SURROUND THIS ONE.

"That sounds like Heaven with extra space," Dr. Childs said, his voice twisted with what felt like disappointment.

AHH, THE ETERNAL AFTERLIFE. IT IS THERE, THOUGH NOT FOR ALL, AND THERE WERE SOME WHO KNEW AND PERVERTED THE MESSAGE FOR THEIR OWN ENDS. GOD IS NOT ONE ENTITY, DR. CHILDS, BUT MANY AND THEY DO NOT CARE FOR YOUR PLANET AS MUCH AS SOME WOULD LIKE THEM TO. AND YET, STILL YOU HESITATE. I WILL TELL YOU THEN, DR. CHILDS, THAT YOUR WORLD IS DOOMED NOT IN THE TIMEFRAME THE INFERIORS HAVE GIVEN, BUT IN YOUR LIFETIME. YOUR WORK IS REDUCED TO A FEW SHORT MONTHS OF YOUR EARTHTIME AND YOU WILL NOT SUCCEED AS YOU WOULD LIKE. I WILL TELL YOU THAT YOU WILL DO

EXACTLY AS YOU HAVE SAID YOU WILL, ALL THOSE MANY EONS AND AGES AND ETERNITIES AGO WHEN YOU SET YOURSELF ON THIS PATH. AND NOW, I SIMPLY REMIND YOU OF WHAT THAT MINISCULE VESSEL HAS FORGOTTEN, THAT YOU HAVE MOVED BEYOND THIS EXISTENCE ONCE BEFORE AND NOW YOU WILL AGAIN, THOUGH THE WORLD MAY BE DIFFERENT AND THE TIME AND THE DOMINANT SPECIES. DOCTOR YOU ARE HERE, HEALER YOU HAVE BEEN, SPIRIT TENDER BEFORE THAT, AND SO ON, THROUGH THE MILENNIA. HERE, TASTE YOUR MAGIC.

The creature's words had swelled and contracted within Dr. Childs and, as it spoke, he had felt something ripping through him though it was beyond pleasure even as he felt shredded and eviscerated. At its last words, the creature swelled and morphed, its shape changing as it formed arms and a head. When it had a vaguely humanoid shape, it leaned over him and breathed down, hard, so that Dr. Childs felt that he was in a hurricane within the empty space around them. The creature's breath was hot with the dust of a thousand million worlds and the vast and full space between them and it blew through Dr. Childs so that he felt as though each atom became the size of the moon. He cried out in terror and ecstasy and his wings, already massive, unfurled and stretched out in the wind, the feathers becoming translucent and then rippling through every shade of color that had ever existed.

The creature stopped blowing and collapsed back into itself but the eye remained open and fixed on Dr. Childs who was sobbing at the return to the now empty and horrifyingly mundane existence of Earth. He thought about his work and job, about parking tickets and childbirth and credit scores and drive thru meals and all of it, every single aspect was lacking and trivial. Behind it all were the sparks of creation that had been packed and trapped in the meat suits of Earth, forced to live through lives that had been largely made meaningless. He wept for the lost potential. The creature blinked.

YOU UNDERSTAND, DR, CHILDS, THAT YOU ARE NOT HERE TO SAVE THEM. YOU ARE HERE TO PUSH THEM ON THEIR WAY. SOME WILL GO, OTHERS WILL STAY AND RELIVE THE CYCLE AND THAT IS THE WAY OF THINGS IN EVERY DARK CORNER OF EVERY UNIVERSE. THOSE THAT FOLLOW, THEY WILL CONTINUE THE MAGIC. THE INFERIORS WILL NOT UNDERSTAND. THEY HAVE CHANGED THEIR BODIES BUT THE MINDS BEHIND THEM ARE FEEBLE AND TOO EARTHBOUND. COME, IT IS TIME. I WILL TAKE US OUT OF HERE THAT YOU MIGHT SPREAD YOUR WINGS AND YOUR MESSAGE AND BRING THOSE THAT WILL GO. THE DESERT OUTSIDE IS WHERE YOU WILL ASCEND INTO THE ETERNITY OF PLANES. ALIGHT ONTO MY BACK.

Dr. Childs had long ago swiped the headphones from his ears, able to understand the creature with no effort. Now, he stepped back slightly as the creature changed again, becoming a massive red-gold dragon. Dr. Childs, using his own wings for a boost, leapt onto the dragons back, his legs and hands sinking slightly within the dragon's skin to keep him seated. Overhead, alarms begin to blare but the dragon only laughed, a massive bellowing sound that echoed into a roar. He took a huge breath and blew it out, launching a stream of molten lava at the ceiling. The lave bored through the ceiling and into the floors above where he could hear panicked screams. At the first hint of daylight through layers of rock and earth, the dragon heaved itself up and flapping its wings, used them to lift himself until he could grab the ceiling and pull them through. He scaled the floors and rock layers like a massive, house-crawling lizard until they were standing on the desert floor. Dr. Childs looked around, somewhat bleary at everything that had transpired yet determined to do what was even now leaking into his conscious mind from submerged memory.

AND NOW, OLD FRIEND, I LEAVE YOU TO YOUR TRUE WORK. I WILL MEET YOU HERE IN TWO MONTHS OF EARTH TIME WHEN THE MOON HIDES

HER FACE. THEN WE WILL ASCEND AND MAKE FOR THE FAR CORNERS OF EXISTENCE.

Dr. Childs leapt from the dragon's back and watched as he heaved himself skyward, his wings drumming the air as he pulled himself up and up and into the blackness of space. The sirens continued below but for Dr. Childs, they were inconsequential. He looked up at the sun, his eyes silvering against the light, and then shook out his own wings, once again the shimmering onyx he was used to, and used them to propel himself into flight. He had practiced, over the years, and was soon expertly winging his way north. There were people to bring to the truth, after all. And he knew of quite a few who would be eager and ecstatic to learn the real truth behind the secrets kept hidden in the Nevada desert. Quite a few indeed.

What in Deer Nation?

Talia turned the corner past her house, her little dog sniffing happily at the grass, when she saw the deer. Immediately stopping in her tracks, Talia felt her heartbeat ratchet up for a moment before she registered that it was just a deer. She was going to cross to the far side of the street to give it some space when she realized it hadn't moved. Her heart clashed again in her chest but she blew out some air through her nose and mentally told herself to get a grip. It was a buck, and they were in full rutting season so not moving was kind of in the job description at this point. Still, something about it unnerved her. It wasn't blinking and didn't seem to be breathing though she *was* looking at it head on and couldn't really tell from the distance. To be on the safer side, Talia turned up a side street instead, looking back once as she and her clueless dog continued their walk with the slight detour.

"I should have gotten a mastiff," she muttered to her pup who looked back at the sound of her voice and wagged his nub of a tail. She smiled at him and took back her words and the walk went as it normally did, which is to say that her dog peed on everything, pooped once which she dutifully collected, and then they went home. As she turned onto that first detour street and got closer to where she would turn toward her house, the deer stepped into the intersection and swung its head to look at her. Talia stopped and this time, so did her dog. He saw the deer and instead of barking as he normally did at anything larger than himself, he cringed backward behind her legs, cowering at her feet.

"Don't you have ladies to find?" she asked the deer, then felt foolish and looked around to see who might have heard her talking to the animal. The street was deserted and, looking back at the deer which was again standing obscenely still, now in the middle of the road, Talia felt that lack of humanity in a very keen and desperate way. She looked through the little patch of woods that obscured her house, then back at the deer, and finally scooped up her little dog who was trembling with fear and pushed her way into the trees. It was a short way from the road to her house but the trees and leafless bushes were a difficult barrier to push through and she was sweating by the time she put the first foot in her yard. Stepping out fully, Talia gasped and fell back a step. The deer was in her driveway, effectively blocking her from getting into her house.

"What the hell, you asshole?" she shouted, fear making her voice tremble as much as her little dog. "Go on, get out of here," she waved a hand toward the deer but it didn't move, simply watched her, unblinking. Talia felt a real grip of fear then. The buck was massive, the kind of specimen that hunters would salivate over and his rack of antlers looked like it could easily rip through her stomach and chest. She looked from the deer to her front door and wondered if she could make it but when the deer dropped his head, looking for all the world like a bull about to charge, her meager courage fled and she wondered if he'd be able to reach her in the woods.

Just then, a truck drove by and she heard the rusty squeal of brakes. A voice, the voice of an angel, really, hollered at her from the driver's side window.

"'Ay girl, you need a hand with that buck?" The older man leaning slightly out of his window was frowning at the deer and Talia felt she could have kissed him, even if he didn't want it.

"Yes! Yes, please! That thing was just in the road so I went around this way but then it was in my yard and he's blocking me…" She trailed off, aware she was babbling but the man simply nodded, backed up slightly, and pulled slowly into her driveway. He angled his truck between her and the deer and laid on his horn. At first, she thought it wouldn't move as it continued to stare at her, not even acknowledging the blaring truck just inches from its face. But when the man drove forward a little more, softly bumping the big animal, it gave a rough snort, shook its head and trotted gracefully away from her and her house. Talia sighed with massive relief and hurried around to the drivers side door.

"Thank you so much! I know they are bold during rutting season but that was a first for me. I was getting pretty scared there!" She beamed up at the man but he was still frowning at the deer as it loped away. He seemed to shake himself and looked down at her.

"Huh? It's not rutting season, girl. That's been gone. Maybe that deer is sick, you oughta keep something with you the next time you walk that little doggy. It might come at you. Weirdest day with these animals," that last was muttered to himself and Talia stepped back as he waved at her and backed his truck back on to the road. She was more than glad he had driven by when he did and she looked toward where the deer had run off but now there was no sign of it. Her little dog still trembled in her arms so she took him inside and locked the door which made her pause since she *never* locked it and really would a deer be able to open a door at all? In the end, she left it locked and then, as days usually do, it progressed to night and by then she had mostly forgotten the morning's strange encounter.

The next day, during her long morning break, Talia started to get her little dog ready for his usual walk. Uncharacteristically, he refused to stand so could put his harness on, running instead to his little bed and rolling to his back when she walked over, his tail wagging but obvious distress in the rest of his body. Talia was confused as he'd never behaved in such a way. She went to her front window and peeked through the curtain but reared back in shock and fear as the deer stared back at her through the glass. The curtain had caught on a chair she kept by the window so she had the perfect view as it slowly and elegantly reared back onto its hind legs and then, with the precision of a ballerina, it drove forward, smashing its hooves and antlers through the glass. Talia screamed and fell backwards to the ground as the massive bulk of it leapt into her house. It stared down at her as she lay with one hand up in a warding off gesture and for nearly a minute the two simply looked at each other. Then, her little dog whimpered in fear as he peed all over his bed and, as if that was the cue it had been waiting on, the deer rushed forward, opened its jaws wide and clamped its teeth over Talia's hand.

Talia had not quite expected that to happen though she was certain that it meant to attack her. Deer don't normally, after all, pirouhette themselves through living room windows. She didn't expect the bite but what was worse was that for some unknown, abnormality of science or mutation or genetic tampering, the deer that currently held its hand in her mouth had teeth like a fucking tiger. As blood poured from its mouth, Talia uttered the shriek that had been stuck in her throat but it choked off into eye-bulging silence as the deer neatly turned its head away in one smooth motion, her hand coming off at the wrist. It chewed once, swallowed neatly and dove forward again but Talia was already scrambling backward, the bloody stump of her right hand slicking the wood floor and making her mad rush backward feel like a nightmare of a fever dream. She screamed again and kicked both legs out as it came at her and then, like the woodcutter of Little Red Riding Hood's dreams, a man leapt through her window and fired a massive shotgun into the side of the deer. It went down with a delicate sigh, its antlered head falling into her lap as Talia, screaming and scrambling, managed to get out from under it. She was still screaming as the man grabbed her, rushed her into the bathroom and clamped a towel over her spirting stump.

She only stopped screaming when he mashed his palm over her mouth. There was no pain yet, strangely, but Talia knew that it would come and it would be huge.

"You have to stop screaming, there are more of them out there. Okay?" Talia processed his words, swallowed her screams, and nodded jerkily. He slowly pulled his hand away from her mouth and Talia kept the screams in though her lips were pulled back from her teeth in a grotesque snarl of shock and adrenaline. She looked over his shoulder at the slumped and bleeding form that lay on her living room floor.

"What is happening?" she managed to juggle out of what felt like a twisted windpipe.

"No idea except that there are massive herds of deer *everywhere* and they're eating people left and right. First aid kit?" Talia goggled at him and then pointed under the sink, watching as he pulled out her thoroughly prepped kit, thank you doomsday documentaries, and began to administer to the stump where, only moments ago, she'd had a perfectly good and functioning hand.

"Take these, get ahead of the pain," he put four aspirin into her open and panting mouth and dribbled water into her mouth to wash it down. Talia swallowed, the pills only sticking for a moment, and then began to cry silently and hideously, as he gauzed and wrapped, gauzed and wrapped, her wrist. When he was done, she had a snow-white club at the end of her wrist and the deeply pulsing ache that would, very soon, metastasize into pain that she didn't want to imagine.

"I'm going to pass out," she told him and started to slump but he grabbed her and seated her on the toilet, slapping her cheeks gently as her eyes fluttered. Eventually, it passed and Talia leaned on the sink, breathing heavily.

"Let's get to my truck, I want to look for anyone else. I've got a cabin we can get to where we'll be safe."

"A cabin. In the woods probably, right? Deer are in the woods, how is that safe?" Talia was slurring her words but she ignored that for the moment.

"It's got a bunker, that's where we can go. Can you stand? I know I heard other people out there but we've got to get moving. I'm telling you, those things are everywhere." Without waiting for her to decide on her own, the man hauled her to her feet, waited a moment while she steadied herself, and then pulled her to the front door. Just as he was opening it, she pulled out of his grasp and hurried over to her little dog.

"Leave the damn thing, we have to *go*."

"I'll never leave him," she admonished the man, aware of the absurdity of her words as she tucked her little dog into her hoodie and zipped it all the way up. He was a comfortable, trembling bulge against her stomach as she followed the man out to his truck. He helped her in and rushed to his side, just shutting the door when something smashed into the side of the truck, rocking it slightly. Talia screamed again but there was only air behind it so that it was instead a silent exhalation of fear. The man cursed heavily and fumbled the keys, smashing the gas to reverse them onto the street just as the deer outside made contact again. She could gear the squeal of bone on metal and then they were racing through her quiet, suburban neighborhood where deer were rushing madly about, trampling bodies on lawns and bellowing through houses.

Ahead of them, a man and a young boy pelted out into the street and the man in the truck slammed his brakes as the boy stumbled to his knees. Behind them, a deer was charging, antlers down and horrific fangs frothing as it aimed for the downed child. The man gunned his truck forward, skirting around the boy and smashing into the deer, sending it rolling back onto the lawn it had come running from. Talia watched wide-eyed as it hauled itself to its feet and, before she could see it try again, the man had thrown open her door and was pushing her over to make room for him and the boy. Both were sobbing wildly as the newcomer slammed his door, grasped the boy and smacked his hand on the dash, the universal sound for 'let's fucking goooooooo!'. Then the truck was hurtling forward again, the deer behind them watching with empty eyes.

They picked up six more people, all of them flinging themselves into the back of the pickup as it slowed in and then they were out of the suburbs and heading to the woods. It took an hour to get to the man's cabin and, though it was still light out, that was fading fast. The traumatized group huddled together, those without wounds helping those who bled or limped, and the man hurried them into his cabin, down a set of side stairs and into a very sophisticated and obviously expensive end-of-days bunker. He then recruited two of the saved to raid the house upstairs for everything they could possibly carry and, only when he was satisfied, did the man close the heavy blast door.

For nearly ten minutes, the only sounds were the gasps, soft cries and sobs of the group as they tried to process what the heck had just happened. Talia put her little dog down and clutched at her arm where the bandage ended. The pain was coming now and it was huge, the aura of it seeming to stretch for miles around the stump of her hand.

"Does anybody know what the *fuck* just happened?" asked the first man they'd found. The young boy, his son she presumed, had buried his face in the man's leg and was crying almost silently. "Did we really, I mean *really* just get attacked by a bunch of deer?"

"Those deer had teeth," one young woman said, her voice quavering with the words. "One of them tore my husband's throat out and ate it." She stopped to bury her face in her hands and sob loudly.

"I've got a radio, hang on and let me see if I can find anything," said the man who owned the bunker. He opened a cabinet further in the room and pulled out a shelf that held radio equipment and began to fiddle with the dials. The group waited, almost holding their breath, as he tried to find a station with news.

Finally, some static and then a reassuring voice that told them all not to panic, that it was under control, that there was nothing to fear. Talia uttered a harsh laugh that hiccupped into a sob which she held back by biting the skin of her good hand. The man with the son was about to speak when another voice came on, this one sounding harried and panicked and not at all like the voice of reason.

"Okay folks, those of you just tuning in I've shut off the recording to bring you live updates. The news we have is not good so I want to start by saying that you absolutely should be off the streets and in your homes or somewhere you can easily barricade. Get to a second floor, block off the stairs, block your doorways, anything you can do to keep them out. Now, I have a statement made by a CDC official just this morning and confirmed by sources within the White House which I'll read to you now. 'Public notice of extreme danger. At 0300 this morning, November the second, twenty thirty-two, the CDC has been made aware of a mutagen within deer populations worldwide. The

mutagen is of an unknown origin at this time and has caused profound changes to both morphology and behavioral aspects of all species of deer. Again, this is a worldwide phenomena with confirmed reports from multiple international governments. As of this time, there is concern of massive casualties due to the mutagen and the violent nature being presented by, again, ALL species of deer in a worldwide phenomenon. The public is encouraged to stay indoors, stay away from windows and easy access points, and try to hang colored cloth from high points of homes or buildings to indicate need for assistance.'" The voice on the radio stopped to clear his throat before continuing.

"Ladies and gentleman, that is a report from the CDC that we received here this morning. Now, it looks as though the president will make an address. Please stay tuned, if you can, to hear this breaking address."

There was some static on the radio and then the president came over the speakers and everyone in the bunker crowded even closer.

"My fellow Americans, at this time, all military forces have been deployed within our borders, as well as worldwide with full cooperation of foreign governments, to contain and eliminate a truly unprecedented event that has gripped deer populations across the globe. The CDC is working diligently and around the clock to identify the cause of the mutagen that has so drastically gripped these animals, resulting in the violent and extremely dangerous behavior that we have seen. Please, I urge caution and for everyone to remain indoors. Those that have the means to protect themselves and others, please do so as it will take time for our military to deploy fully. I assure you all that we are working swiftly and with precision and serious intent to curb the threat that has sprung up in our midst. Keep your radios close, help each other, and by all means, please stay safe. We are on the way."

The presidents voice cut out and the radio went silent causing a mild uproar to occur. The man who owned the bunker fiddled with the dials but nothing came again from the speakers.

"We'll wait, maybe it will come back on. For now, let's get those who need medical care back to the barracks I have here. I've got full medical kits and then we can get some food going. Right now, let's take care of the basics and leave later for later." Talia stood and followed the injured back to where clean beds were set up in a warm room. She took one in the middle of the room and laid down, her little dog jumping up to curl on her legs. Talia thought she might sleep but the throbbing sickness of her missing hand was too great and she lay with her eyes squeezed shut, tears leaking through the lids. A hand on her shoulder pulled her eyes open and she looked up into the concerned face of one of the women who had scrambled into the back of the truck.

"Let's take a look, shall we? Lucky for you, I'm a nurse when there aren't monster deer rampaging through the streets."

Talia smiled wanly at the woman's attempt at humor and sat up slowly, her pup shifting to lie beside her. The woman handed her a pill and a glass of water and she looked up, the question on her face.

"It's morphine. It will take a little while to kick in but it will certainly help with the pain. I'll give you another in four hours and after that, we'll see how you feel." Talia nodded and downed the pill then sucked in a slow, deep breath as the woman began to carefully inspect the bandage over her arm. It wasn't too dirty and the ties held so she simply nodded and helped Talia lay back down. "Let's look at it tomorrow and let it rest today, alright?"

"I'm fine with that," Talia said faintly, letting the woman drag the blanket up over her and her pup before she moved on to the next bed. Talia cupped her remaining hand over her little dog's back, letting his thrumming warmth seep into her and, exhausted and spent, she fell into restless sleep.

Excited voices dragged her from sleep and she blearily sat up and looked around. The pain in her stump had faded to a dull, burning ache which was close enough to the cramps she got on her period that she could push it to the background of her mind. She swung her legs out of the bed, helping her pup untangle from the blankets. He was alert and unafraid which quieted the sick thumping of her heart. Talia hauled herself to her feet and went to see what the commotion was about. She found most of the group in a living room area clumped around a television set and she moved closer to see what had captivated everyone.

The screen looked like a war zone or a very accurate action movie. A cameraman, more brave than anyone she could imagine, was following closely behind a group of soldiers who were firing heavily into a herd of deer that was rushing at them. Rockets and grenades and explosions were going off, seemingly at random, and she could see clumps of deer being savaged and thrown by the assault. Still, the numbers seemed overwhelmingly in favor of the formally docile herbivores until a tank rolled into view, and then a second and third, and began firing into the herd.

"TV came on an hour ago," the man told her, his smile wide and satisfied at the carnage on the screen. Talia could only nod before she turned back, mesmerized by the sight of blood and limbs and heads flying every which way. The firing ceased and the smoke cleared and it looked like the soldiers had won, beating back the newly carnivorous creatures. But then the camera whirled, the cameraman screamed and a flood of deer hit the soldiers and tanks from the side. The camera dropped to the ground, bounced a moment, and then focused on the open, unseeing eyes of a dead soldier which were crushed a moment later by a stomping hoof.

"Clever girl," Talia muttered, feeling hysteria bubble up into her throat. The room was now silent and when the screen went black, no one moved to fiddle with the tv.

"Now what?" someone asked, defeat heavy in their voice.

"Now nothing, they'll either kill them all or they won't. For now, let's feed those who slept through dinner, get this place cleaned up, and get some sleep. Later is for later." Talia wondered how often he said that and if he had any other little quips he might come up with. For now, despite the carnage on the screen and her hurting stump, dinner sounded good and she knew her pup would want to eat. She let the group lead her to the dining area and helped herself to two plates of food, one of which she filled with things her dog would eat. The two of them ate and were joined shortly after by the young boy who had stopped crying but had a shell-shocked expression on his face. He watched her dog eat on the floor beside her chair and let his father feed him. Talia looked up at his father.

"They got his mother. Before we even knew what was happening. I mean, I still don't know, but she was just in the garden. They both were. A normal morning and then it was ripping…" he trailed off and fed his son another piece of bread.

"One got my hand," Talia said, lifting the wrapped stump. Both pairs of eyes swiveled to the white lump and then looked down. Talia felt she understood. They didn't have to carry the stump of their mother and wife around, at least. "Did you see them? Before, I mean. Before they started attacking. I saw one in the road, just staring at me. It cut me off from my house and a man in a truck scared it off. Then the next morning it jumped through my window and ate my hand and the man who—who owns this place—"

"Clive," the man said, and Talia paused before nodding.

"Clive. He was there and he blasted it. But, it ate my hand." The last was whispered and Talia looked down at her plate, pushing the food around. She took a bite and looked up and shrugged. "I've always liked deer. This feels like a betrayal, somehow."

"Right? That's what I'm saying!" The father became animated at her words, almost agitated and he jerked slightly in his seat, causing his son to pull away from him. "I mean, *deer* of all things? When there are so many predators? This has to be planned. No one would suspect deer, no one would bat an eye to see them even in the middle of a big city. Someone did this, released these things and now just look."

"Who would do that?" Talia asked, alarmed at the direction the conversation was going. "What sense does that even make? Deer attacking people around the world? For what purpose?"

"It's gotta be ecoterrorists. They've been yapping about climate change for as long as I can remember but the water levels evened out, temperatures evened out, heck, even the polar bears made a comeback."

"Yeah but why then would this be something they'd want to do?"

"Overpopulation. It's so obvious. Remember back in like twenty twenty-two when the world hit eight billion people and everyone said it was going to be the end soon? Well, now we're at, what, sixteen billion? And we've got it figured out. But some people, they just think there are too many people. This is population control, mark my words."

"Ecoterrorists aren't the ones traditionally involved with population control, though. Isn't that the governments stomping grounds?"

"Okay, fine, the government then. But they're working with these groups, guaranteed." The man sat back, satisfied with his argument and gave his son another bite of bread. Talia looked down at her plate, surprised to see that she'd finished everything while the unhinged discussion had been happening.

"Maybe it's just aliens," she offered and then stood up and collected her and her dog's plates, balancing them awkwardly in her good hand. She nodded to the man and took her plates to the kitchen, annoyed that there were still these idiotic conspiracies floating around. She thought all the nuts had been stamped out. Twenty twenty-two had been a breaking point for the world but instead of sliding back into the same shit that had dragged everyone to that point, enough people finally said 'enough' and, shockingly for everyone, world governments got their shit together and made massive changes for the better. The man was right, water levels had stopped rising, ocean temperatures had leveled out leading to a surge in fish and ocean mammal populations. Mega-storms had stopped devastating massive areas and, overall, life on the Earth had gotten pretty good. The US had even gotten rid of credit scores which Talia thought was the greatest achievement of all. So why this nutty idea about a conspiracy of carnivorous, violent deer? Talia tried to let it go but the thought stayed with her, aching in her brain like the ache of her stump and, as she lay back down in her bed, little dog curled at her side, she thought about it some more.

The next morning, she sought out the man and his son and, finding them again in the dining room, this time surrounded by other people, Talia pulled a chair close to him and sat down.

"I think you're right," she told him and conversation around them stopped.

"About what?" he asked, put off by her intensity.

"Remember the president saying, and that CDC briefing that the guy read, saying that it was an 'unknown mutagen'?"

"Yes?"

"How would they know it's a mutagen? I mean, why even use that word?"

"Well, the deer are obviously mutated," one of the women at the table offered but she looked like she was thoroughly invested in what Talia was beginning to say out loud and she clapped her jaw shut and leaned forward.

"Sure, that's obvious to all of us. I mean, deer don't have sharp teeth. Anyway, mutagen is such a weird word to use, right? They could have said virus, or bacteria, or even, like, unknown anomaly and that would make sense. But 'unknown mutagen' sounds like what you would say when you *know* what caused something but want to make it sound like you don't actually know."

"But why? And who would do this?"

"It's obviously the world governments," the man said, getting into the argument. "Sixteen billion people is too many, no matter how efficient the world has gotten."

"But there aren't problems anymore, not anything like there used to be with homelessness and world hunger and all that," the same woman said, clearly working her role as devil's advocate.

"Look, I read an article from a leading medical journal that said that seventeen billion people would be the absolute tipping point for the planet. I read it on a Monday and by Tuesday it had been erased from everywhere, even the internet which shouldn't be possible. We'll reach seventeen billion by next year, guaranteed. Except, not if the government releases hybrid deer to kill off a huge percentage of the population."

"Okay, but *deer*? I mean, come on," one of the men said, skepticism heavy in his arms-crossed posture.

"I said it last night, what better way to sneak something in? We'd all notice if the streets were suddenly overrun by tigers, right? But deer? They're already everywhere, it's easy to flood the ranks and let them do what they've been programmed to do."

There were nods and looks of comprehension on the faces gathered at the table but when a voice behind them suddenly guffawed loudly, everyone whirled and changed to sheepish and embarrassed. The man who owned the bunker, Clive, was standing in the doorway, a big grin on his face as he surveyed everyone.

"You don't think there's a point to the argument?" Talia challenged him, feeling her stump begin to thump with pain as her heart rate increased at the confrontation.

"Uh, no, not even with the collective way the world has suddenly managed to run so smoothly. They're calling it mutagen because someone at the CDC already figured that out, guaranteed." He winked at the father whose brow furrowed with annoyance. "There is no way on this green earth that any government would throw its armed forces in the path of something like this if they're the ones who created and released it. They'd need all hands on deck for the aftermath and to maintain control in the face of overwhelming loss and panic on the part of the public."

"Well, what is it then if you know so much," Talia flung at him, cradling her burning arm.

"It's an invasion force," he replied simply, looking hard at her.

"An invasion force," one of the men said flatly. "Of what? Aliens?"

"Not any aliens we've ever conceived of."

"What are you even talking about?" Talia asked, the pain now sneaking into her shoulder.

"Do y'all remember when that forest was found that turned out to be just one tree? I mean that it was a huge forest, covered hundreds of square miles but all the trees were connected and, genetically, it was one organism?"

Everyone began nodding reluctantly but Talia was suddenly wary of the way the man was talking. He seemed like a backwoods rural type, complete with overalls and thick southern accent so his sudden words prickled at the back of her head.

"Okay, well, it turns out, that "forest" didn't originate on this planet. A botanist found the initial tree and sequenced the genome. It has DNA unlike anything that exists here. Though I bet if they sequence these deer, they'll find something similar."

"That forest isn't killing people though, the logic doesn't track."

"It's not killing people but it's spreading and killing everything else. No other plants or trees grow in that forest."

"An invasion force decades in the making? What kind of alien species would wait that long?" Talia asked but broke off as the pain flared and began to spread down her back.

"One that has time to get here, one that can spread easily over the years." The man who owned the bunker was standing over her now and Talia hadn't realized he'd moved, she was too preoccupied with the pain in her body.

"I need some more morphine, I think. My hand might be infected."

"Your hand is gone, girl. Why don't we take look." Clive grabbed the bandage and began to unwind it. Something told Talia to make him stop but she couldn't look away from the slowly shrinking bandage. When he got to the last few layers, everyone had crowded around and were looking in amazement and no little fear as the outline of a hand was clearly visible. He unwound it fully and Talia looked on with the others at a hand where there had been none, though there was something wrong with it.

"Why is it moldy?" the little boy asked, his first words in days, and the fear in his voice caused everyone to back away from Clive and Talia.

"Looks like the invasion is spreading," Clive said softly.

"You knew this would happen, didn't you? You knew about all of this." Talia looked up at him with something like wonder on her face and Clive, blinking slowly, simply shrugged.

"It was only a matter of time, really, for this to all start. All the signs were there and it would have happened sooner except that someone high up figured it out too. Some of it, anyway."

"Why did you bring her here if you knew that?" the boy's father shouted, grabbing his son close. "What's happening? Are we all infected like that?"

"By now, yes."

"What?!" Everyone began yelling and clamoring to get away, tears and panic pouring off of them.

"QUIET!" Clive roared, settling the room immediately into gasping silence. "It was only a matter of time anyway, all I've done is give us somewhere safe to transition. The deer-things were not meant to be a catalyst to change, that much is obvious by the way they've decimated humanity. This change, and others I've seen, is something unexpected. For us, and for them I imagine."

"How can you even know something like that? How can you know that this change won't kill us or turn us into monsters or…look at her hand! She looks like old bread!"

"Your fear and panic are clouding your judgement. It's obvious to anyone with half a brain cell what's going on. This planet has been successfully infiltrated, colonization has begun, and soon there will be a new dominant species. I intend to remain in that category. This," he held up Talia's new hand, "is how we get there."

"I'm outta here," the man said, pulling his son with him. "I'd rather take my chances with those deer then sit in this bunker and wait for who knows what's next. Are you going to stop us?" He had stopped at the door to the dining room, chin held up defiantly though all could see the way it quavered.

"No, I won't stop you. Please wait for me to open the door though, so that I can lock it behind you. Anyone that wants is welcome to take a pack from the front closet, they're full of food and survival gear. In twenty minutes I'll open the door for those wanting to leave. After that, I'm shutting it until all of this is over. Think hard about what you want folks. Outside is certain death."

Twenty minutes later only three people had packs on their backs and were waiting by the door. Talia was hanging back but she saw that the father didn't have his son. He was clearly distraught but obviously determined to leave and she wondered what had happened to make the man okay with leaving his son. Fear was a powerful motivator, apparently. Clive looked all three in the eyes and held their gazes before nodding and moving to open the door. They all breathed in the rush of air that flooded the room but there was apprehension and no small amount of terror hanging over the group as well. She suspected they all had a moment of expecting a herd of deer to rampage through the door. When nothing happened, the three walked through the doorway and up the stairs and Clive closed the door on their backs. The final seal of the door was like a release and the small group, now even smaller, dispersed. Talia went to find her dog.

He was on her bed, the boy beside him, and in obvious bliss as he was getting scratches on scratches. Talia sat on the other side and looked down at her new, old-looking hand.

"Your dog is changing too, but he's still nice," the boy said into the silence. Talia looked at him and then down at her pup and saw that sure enough, he was different. His tail nub was now much longer and she realized that he was bigger as well. She rolled him over and looked at his face, surprised at the deep intelligence she could see there. Her dog was studying her even as she studied him and when he nudged her hand, she stroked him with it.

"He doesn't care what it looks like," Talia said as she ran her new hand along his back.

"That's why dogs are the best," the boy said sadly. Talia nodded. The boy reached out and began to pet her pup again and

Talia noticed a spot along his arm that matched her hand. She touched it with one finger.

"That's where he was licking me when I was petting him yesterday. That's why I didn't go with my dad. I hope we aren't gross, in the end, like those deer." He sighed and stood up, giving the dog one last pat before wandering out of the barracks room. Talia laid back on the bed and held her dog when he curled up at her side. He was not thrumming with fear anymore so she decided that she wouldn't either. She clenched her new fist and fell asleep.

Talia dreamed, through a curtain of whitish-green, that she was aboard a ship, one of countless, that was nearly at planet Earth. On board, where she would expect to see confines of metal and steam and piping, was rather a lush and breathing forest. Through the forest, glided willowy beings with skin the color of her hand. Hairless, ephemeral, with the grace of years-long ballerinas, the creatures danced around each other, baring sharp fangs in greeting and trilling fluting hoots to each other as they slid through space. In her sleep, Talia's hand moved with the same grace as it danced through the air over the bed and, in her dream, she thought that it would be a nice change to be so tall.

Outside, and far overhead, countless ships bore down on Earth, the inhabitants ready to begin their population of a planet that they had seeded with life so long ago.

Snow Storm

The massive solar storm was expected, anticipated, and so all precautions were taken, though in the end it was all unnecessary as there was very little in the way of disruption. Multiple countries' residents reported an odd, low-pitched hum that lasted two days and the entirety of Earth's sky, every hemisphere, was witness to dazzling and vibrant aurora displays. The storms dissipated, the aurora and hum faded, and everything went back to business as usual until an arctic research center began to report a surge in snowpack and the 'regrowth' of previously shrinking glaciers. More research centers investigated, experts were called in, and months after the first reports, it was confirmed that ice melt was no longer a problem. Antarctica began to report the same data the next year and, all around the globe, people who had no idea what was happening but who took the credit anyway, shook hands all around, and patted their own backs. Two years later, the first winter storms began and it was then that humanity began to realize there was actually a problem, one that looked to be far more devastating than anyone could have predicted.

"I *got* bread Sharon, Jesus! I got four loaves, how many more do you want? Didn't you already make six sourdough yesterday? I think we're okay to wait out a two day snowstorm."

"They're calling this one 'once in a generation' Harold. I'm not taking any chances."

"They say that about every one of these bastards. Just want to scare the tourists I bet. We're fine, we could last two years with everything we've got in the cellar."

If you think so…" Sharon trailed off. Harold shook his head but went outside to check the firewood stack anyway. Every year there was a big snowstorm at this time and every year the weather folks made a big deal of nothing. Harold began moving more wood to the mudroom, making a second layer and Sharon made no comment while he did. She knew he was worried, just as she was, they'd both been glued to the weather station each evening watching the front develop. It looked nasty on the screen and Sharon went to the cellar again just to reassure herself. It was a food stock that she was particularly proud of, with floor to ceiling shelves along every wall and two aisles in the middle, all stocked with food she'd been canning and storing for three years. She ran her fingers along the shelves and then checked the dog food bins to make sure the mice hadn't been able to get in at the bags. She and Harold had four very beloved bloodhounds and they were fully stocked as well.

"Honey," Harold's voice called down to her and the choked horror in it made her rush up the cellar steps, something she'd never done. Harold was standing in the living room, tv remote in hand as he stared at the screen. Sharon turned to look and her hand crept up to her throat. The storm front had more than tripled in size and the meteorologist was no longer showing the local area. They had panned out and out on the map to show a projection that covered the entirety of the northern hemisphere and across the equator as well. Even as they watched, the projection continued to expand. It was forecast to start any minute and while temperatures weren't particularly low, into the 20's, the projected snowfall was reading in feet.

"I'm going to run in for gas for the generator. What else do we need?" The trembling panic in Harold's voice threatened to overwhelm Sharon but she took a deep breath and looked at her husband and then at the four dogs who were watching them intently, no longer snoring away on the couch.

"We have everything Harold, but," she grabbed his hand. "Get me a doughnut, will you?" He smiled weakly at her and then rushed to grab his jacket and keys. Their eldest dog, Harold's favorite, tried to follow him out but Harold shooed him back in and left, leaving Sharon and the dogs to wait anxiously for his return.

He'd been gone twenty minutes when the snow started and thirty minutes after that it was nearly whiteout conditions. Sharon was pacing, terrified by then, as Harold should have been back.

She was about to grab her coat and try to go find him when headlights splashed through the windows and the familiar sound of his truck cut through her fear. She let out a small, relieved cry and she and the dogs rushed out to meet him. Harold was hauling two full cans of gasoline into the small shed that held their generator and he nodded at Sharon's anxious waving. Two minutes later he was stomping the snow from his boots on the porch and then letting in a blowing gust of wind and snow as he rushed inside.

"It's bad," was all he said, terse and unhappy, as he hung his jacket.

"We have enough to last, Harold. I'm not worried."

"It's not the food, Sharon, that I'm worried about. There's almost no one out. The gas station was closed so I couldn't grab anything, I'm just glad they left the pumps on. Let's see what the news is saying." He brushed past her, giving her a quick squeeze on the shoulder, and she followed him into the living room where he began flipping through the channels to find local news. A reporter's voice filled the room when he stopped.

"*...urging people to stay in their homes. This is classified as a level three emergency with special precautions and is expected to be an extended event. Again, we urge everyone to please stay indoors and off the roads. Emergency services do not expect to be able to reach anyone experiencing an emergency in a timely manner. Again, we are in a level three emergency with special precautions and conditions are expected to worsen considerably within the next two hours.*"

Harold shut off the news and sat heavily on the couch, the dogs crowding around him.

"Harold, we had a level three in '92. Why are you scared?" Sharon did not mean the words as a rebuke and Harold could hear the trembling fear in her voice as he looked up at her.

"There's something in the snow," he said finally, darkly.

"Something...like hail?"

"*Things,* Sharon. There are things in the snow."

"Plastic? Food coloring, leprechauns? What things, Harold, what does that even mean? What a stupid thing to say." She was near hysteria now, unnerved and terrified by Harold's tense and uncharacteristic demeanor.

"Okay," he said, getting up and folding her in his arms. "Okay, let's relax a minute and take a breath." To punctuate his words, he took a deep, trembling breath that steadied as he blew it out. Sharon copied him and they spent several moments breathing deeply as he held her. Inside the house, it was quiet and calm, but outside they could hear the wind picking up and the hissing deluge of snow on the roof. Sharon looked out the front window and was shocked to see what looked already like a foot of snow at the edge of the deck, piling against the railing. A shadow moving across the window made her gasp and jerk back and, on the couch, the dogs all bristled and came alert, emitting a chorus of quiet growls as they looked out the window. Harold looked at them and then at her, glanced out the window and moved to close the shutters.

"Get the windows Sharon, lock them up. I'll get these and the ones upstairs. Go, now!" he shouted when she didn't move right away. His sharp command sent her scuttling to the kitchen and she unlatched the thick, heavy shutters that Harold had insisted they install when the first hurricane had reached all the way up to their neck of the woods. She had questioned why they didn't put them on the outside of the house, which seemed typical, and he'd replied he didn't want to risk being outside to close them with hurricane winds chapping his ass. Sharon was faintingly grateful for that now as she closed the shutters and locked down both of the heavy bars. Hurrying now, she raced through the first floor shuttering all the windows as, above her, Harold closed up the second floor. She also heard him slam the attic door bar into place and a thick shudder of nauseating fear rippled through her.

The dogs were at her feet the whole way, ears swiveling at every sound of the house being locked down but then, as one, their heads whipped to the front door and Sharon, standing at the kitchen island, listened in horror as something scraped along the door. The dogs were silent but fixated on the door, hackles raised. Sharon could hear Harold coming down the stairs and then she was moving, skidding across the kitchen floor in her socks. She reached the door and slammed the bolt home before pushing the door bar down into the floor. The scraping sound came again and with her breath caught sharply in her throat, Sharon heard a low, slobbering moan filter through the thick wood of the door. She moaned softly in response and backed away. Behind her came Harold, his rifle trained on the door and she moved behind him to the dogs who pushed their bodies close to hers. Still, they made no noise, even when that horrific moan came again.

"What is it?" Sharon whispered, hands creeping to her ears. "Oh my god, the back door." Harold turned to her, eyes wide, and she spun and hurtled to the back of the house. The door was shut and she almost sobbed in relief but the sound died in a choke in her throat as a shadow loomed through the frosted glass which covered half the door. Without thinking, Sharon lunged forward and, grabbing the shutter door in both hands, she slammed it and threw the lock bars down just as the glass on the other side shattered. A bellowing roar ripped through the wood and she felt the door tremble under her hands.

"Sharon!" she could hear Harold's panicked cry as he rushed toward her.

"I got it," she sobbed. "It's shut, I got it." He came around the corner just as something big landed on their roof. The door behind them shuddered again and now there was pounding all around the house.

"Get downstairs, now. Let's go." He grabbed her hand and hauled her toward the cellar, calling the dogs as they went. The six of them raced through the house to the kitchen and Harold pushed her and the dogs through the door, pulling it shut behind them as he followed. He locked it and dropped the heavy oak beam, a quirky feature that had come with the house and they'd decided to keep. Sharon squeezed her eyes shut on the tears flowing down her cheeks and thanked every deity she could think of that they had prepared so well for something that no one could have possibly prepared for.

When the lights cut off, Sharon bit back a scream and heard Harold rummaging along the shelves. A small click in the darkness led to a pale illumination as one of the many light sources they'd stored down here came on. The dogs were huddled in a corner, their faces tense and whale-eyed with panic as they panted their fear. Sharon felt terrible for them as they understood less than she did about what was going on and was glad that they, who were normally so vocal, were silent in their terror. She went to them, dropping to her knees on the hard cement and pulled them close, feeling them lean into her.

"'Things' you said, Harold. Not monsters."

"I don't know what they are, Sharon. There was a screen on the gas pump turned to a national news channel and they were talking about things in the snow, showed grainy footage like those bullshit bigfoot photos. Looked like things."

"What did the news say?" she asked, turning to sit so the dogs could crowd into her lap.

"Nothing helpful. Just to stay in, lock the doors, keep away from windows."

"Well we've done that," she said with a short, bitter laugh. "What should we do next?"

"I don't hear anything anymore," he said after a moment of silent listening. "Where's that radio?" He move to where she pointed, the rifle still firmly in his grasp, and pulled the radio out, setting in on a little table near where she was sitting. After fiddling with the knobs for a moment, the sight of which made Sharon clamp her jaw shut on a brief burst of hilarity as she thought of every scary movie she'd seen with actors doing the same thing, a clear voice came through.

"*…been snowing here six hours and we're up to four feet. From what I can see on this weather app, it's going to keep going another two days at least…holy shit another one!*" The sharp excitement on the man's voice coming through the radio made them jump.

"Folks, if you've seen these things, you know the nightmares I'll be having for months. Oh here comes one of the National Guard units and they have reduced that thing to a pile of meat." Sharon found herself leaning closer, desperate to hear anything that would explain the sudden madness that came with the snow. *"Alright, for those just tuning in, I've got the inside scoop at WX103.3 and a front row seat courtesy of the bullet proof glass installed after last year's shooting.*

"We're being attacked and it's not by a foreign nation. The snow brought something with it and from what I can see, the National Guard are getting their money's worth. We've got tanks and trucks and squads and squads of soldiers rolling through and the monster bodies are piling up folks, though from what I can tell, there seem to be an endless supply of these things. Now, I can't confirm this report, the internet, ya know? But I've gotten hints here and there that these things have been cooking up north

but not by us, or any other government. All those years we caused the glaciers and snowpack to shrink let something out and it spent its time growing. Apparently, that solar storm a few years ago gave them just what they needed on their little evolutionary journey and now we've got full-blown monsters roaming the snow out here folks. Likely many of you have seen what we've seen and let me tell ya, they are nightmare fuel. The good news is that they are not invincible and not even very durable with a few rounds in the chest. So, grab those guns you've got stashed under the bed and load up for bear. Or for monster, I should say. Stay out of the snow, whatever you do, and dump a few rounds in any of these S.O.B.'s that you see. We can get through this folks, the military is coming so just hang on."

The radio cut out but not from the feed going. Sharon saw the power light shut off and got up to help Harold look for more batteries. The pounding and thumping seemed to have stopped but neither of them moved up the stairs to check for sure. The little that Sharon had seen of the snow creatures made her very enthusiastic about remaining in the relative safety, so far, of the cellar. After several minutes of searching, Harold threw up his hands.

"Well now we know we need batteries," he said, exasperation heavy in his voice.

"We got a lot of information with that little bit we heard though. If we stay down here, we should be okay right?"

"I suppose. Oh wait! I've got my phone." He pulled out his cell and Sharon, crowding over his shoulder, was gratified to see the signal and wifi were still working. Harold opened his browser and checked the mainstream sites first but there was little in the way of actual information. Much of it was headlines from the previous day and, when they did find something relevant and recent, it gave essentially the same information they'd heard on the radio.

"What's his 'inside scoop'?" Sharon asked, quietly scoffing. "Try Reddit," she said suddenly and Harold gave her an odd look. "What?" she asked.

"How do you even know what that is?"

"Julianne told me about it, it's where I get new ideas for the garden. Oh my god, call Julianne!" she almost shouted, grabbing for the phone.

"Okay, stop! I will, stop grabbing it. They're fine, they live in Phoenix."

"Harold, that snow went down into South America. Call her now." He batter her hands away and found their daughter's number in the contacts, turning it to speakerphone once it started dialing as Sharon hissed at him to do so. It rang four times and Harold began to fear the worst when their daughter's breathless voice answered.

"Dad? Dad, you're okay? Where's mom, how are you guys. Oh my god…" she dissolved into loud tears and Harold resisted the urge to roll his eyes. Julianne was pragmatic and logical most times but when she was especially stressed, she often became incapable of anything but tears. There was a muffled scuffle and then the tears were in the background and another voice began talking.

"Hey grandpa, we're okay. Are you guys?"

"Oh Timothy!" Sharon sobbed but Harold shushed her.

"Tim, we're okay, we're in the cellar. Where are you guys, you're safe?"

"Yeah, we were at the mall when the snow started and there are a bunch of us in one of the outdoor stores. They have a heavy shelter, an old bomb shelter or something but it's been really decked out. Mom said it's probably illegal, especially for where it's at but those things can't get in."

"You saw them?"

"Yeah they came in right away once the snow got just a few inches. They busted through and killed a bunch of people."

"Oh Tim, you saw that?" Harold felt his heart break for the trauma but Tim made a negative sound.

"Nah, mom made us run as soon as the glass broke plus we were down the mall from it, right by the outdoor place. I heard people screaming though and another older guy said there was dead people all over." Sharon was weeping silently and Harold felt tears threaten as well. He loved his grandson and daughter dearly and was upset he couldn't be there with them. He heard Julianne speaking. "Mom wants to talk to you now. Love you grandma and grandpa." They told him they loved him and then their daughter was there and though they could hear the tears thick in her throat, she sounded calmer when she spoke.

"You're really okay?" she asked.

"Yes, all of us. Even the dogs." Harold heard her heavy exhale. "You are both okay as well? You're safe where you're at?"

"Yes, seems like," came her even reply. "Some of them tried to get in but they didn't try very hard and it's been quiet for a few hours."

"We noticed that here," Harold told her. "They smashed a window and rattled the doors a bit but now we don't hear anything."

"Is it still snowing there?" Julianne asked. "There are small window slits high in the wall and we can see still so much snow coming down."

"I'll check the window, here Sharon," Harold handed the phone to his wife and moved to the wall which held a single window the size of a sheet of paper. He had to climb a step ladder to see through it and, at first, all he could see was a field of white. Slowly he was able to make out the shapes of trees further back and then the side of the shed though the snow was piling nearly to the roof. He was grateful for once for the overhang of the porch on this side of the house as there was a constant vortex of air rushing past this spot. He had cursed it countless times as it either froze him in the winter or blasted heated air in the summer. Now, though, the constant rush of wind kept the window swept clear of snow.

A shadow followed by a dark shape rushed past the window and Harold jumped back off the ladder, landing hard and hissing at the flare of pain in his knee.

"What is it?" Sharon cried out in a harsh whisper-scream. He could hear Julianne on the asking as well.

"It's still snowing and those things are there. One just ran by the window."

"What are they doing?" came Julianne's voice from the phone, hysteria bubbling up. There was a hard rustle on the phone and then her quiet sobbing came from further away as Tim got back on the phone.

"Grandpa, there's something going on outside here. Some of the guys have been going out to check on things and they came back and said the snow is falling thicker than ever and there's a lot of movement outside. What should we do?"

For a moment, Harold was at a total loss. He had his gun and extra ammo but what could he do from thousands of miles away? He felt tears threaten and swallowed hard, forcing them back. He thought of his daughter and grandson, trapped in a mall, while an unknown number of *things* prowled outside.

"Hide," he said finally, his voice dropping. "Take me off speaker, Tim." When Tim assured him it was off, Harold spoke in a low tone. "You and your mother get somewhere to hide. Find a storeroom, a crawlspace, even a door to a maintenance section behind the walls. You need to get somewhere, just the two of you, away from the crowd you're with. Can you do that?"

"Yeah I think so," came the boys reply, his voice trembling slightly. His voice dropped to a whisper. "There's a small door, like a play door almost, that I found earlier. I looked inside and it was a little hallway with pipes and things."

"Good, get in there, you and your mother, and try not to let anyone see you. And do it quick. Also, put the phone on silent and mute the screen glow. I want you to get to a dark place and wait there, okay?"

"Yeah okay, we will."

"Good, and Tim? We love you okay? You can call us when you're safe or even…even, you know, if you're not and want to—want to talk."

Sharon put her hands over her mouth at Harold's words, tears flowing again.

"Okay grandpa, I love you guys."

"We love you too," Harold's voice was thick with unshed tears. "Now get through that door and you hide, you got me?"

"Yes," came his simple reply and then the line went silent and Sharon wailed as she grabbed her husband. He wrapped his arms around her, tears flowing fast and hot, until the first ominous creaking came from the door at the top of the cellar stairs. In the corner, the dogs began to whine in fear and Harold stepped close to look. He could see, through the thin line between the door and the cellar landing, shadows moving in the kitchen. The creaking came again and Harold realized that the door was bowing in the frame. He uttered a quiet curse and turned and pushed his wife toward the coal chute. She was grabbing him, whispering 'no' over and over but he didn't let up. He opened the door, called the dogs over and they went in easily, tails between their legs, before pushing Sharon through. She scrabbled at his arm but he shook her off and pushed her until she fell onto her butt with a shocked grunt.

"I love you more than I would ever have been able to tell you. Lock this when I close it, Sharon, I mean it." He tossed the phone to her in the small space, grabbed two water jugs by the wall and tossed them in at her feet and then shut the door. He could hear her muffled wailing in the small, cramped space. A space not big enough for all of them and he would not leave his dogs out to face whatever nightmare was coming, not when they were so obviously terrified. He had seen these same dogs chase off a black bear with cubs and, once, a massive mountain lion but they had become terrified puppies in the face of whatever nightmare they smelled from the monsters in the snow. Harold waited until he heard Sharon lock the chute door and then moved to the side and began to pile up boxes and crates which he knelt behind. He had a clear view of the cellar door and he placed his rifle on the makeshift cover he'd created, laying his shells out in a line at his knee. Then, he waited.

When the door yielded to whatever was on the other side, it did so with a quiet, almost comical, popping of the lock and bar and the door swung wide. Harold sighted on the hulking form in the doorframe and, before it could lift its head to sniff the air, he fired. His shot went through the things throat and it dropped with a gurgling hiss, its arms drumming the floor for a moment before it lie still. Harold kept his rifle up and ready but it was difficult to keep his hands steady. The creature had too many arms and he had seen what looked like sabretooth teeth in its head before he fired. From the kitchen, outside the doorframe, he began to hear an odd, trilling hum that seemed to come from everywhere in the house. Harold took a deep breath, let it out, and focused on the tip of his rifle. When movement caught his eye at the side of the door, he shifted slightly, focusing his eyes and, when a head came into view, he fired, gratified to watch a large chunk of the top of the creatures head disappear. It dropped with a heavy thump and now the trilling hum had become something else, something angry and wild.

Just as the new sounds, high-pitched squeals and growls, reached a frenzied pitch, they were cut off by a horrific squealing groan coming from the upper floor. Harold looked at the ceiling above him and turned to dive under the metal fireplace in one corner of the cellar. Moments later, the roof of the house collapsed and the shuddering implosion caused much of the first floor ceiling to fall as well. The angry creature sounds were gone and, after several minutes of the house falling in on itself, the only sounds were the heavy hiss of snow coming into the exposed rooms and the slow, tapering groans of what sounded like dying exhalations. Those soon died away and Harold could hear only his own labored breathing.

A hesitant tapping caught his attention and he pulled himself out from under the stove and hurried to open the coal door. Sharon wept when she saw his face and the dogs came wriggling out, ecstatic to see him and be free of the cramped confines. Harold put a finger to his lips and helped Sharon to her feet before moving to stand in front of her. He held the rifle ready as he moved to the bottom of the stairs, his oldest dog stepping in front of him to move cautiously up the stairs, his wrinkled nose sniffing furiously. When he stepped through the doorway and continued into the kitchen, Harold felt safe enough following and soon they were all standing in the ruins of the kitchen.

"Harold," Sharon whispered, one trembling hand latching onto his forearm. He looked where she pointed and saw one of the creatures lying in a mess of wood and snow and their heavy, clawfoot bathtub. It had been crushed, mostly, but they had a clear view of its head and several pairs of arms. Up close and in the light, Harold felt faint as he looked at it.

He had been right about the teeth; this close they were far more terrifying and there were too many of them. He was reminded of a documentary he'd seen once where there had been close up footage of a shark's mouth, the teeth growing every which way. He couldn't imagine being caught by one of those, didn't want to imagine what those teeth could do. Sharon was gripping the back of his shirt and the dogs, though they were trembling with fear, were not cowering as they had been. The youngest, a massive red boy, was stretching his neck toward the thing to sniff at it.

"What are we doing Harold? We can't stay here right? But we can't go out there." Sharon's breath was hitching and, for a moment, Harold had no idea what to do. He looked out through the ruined portion of the house to where the snow continued to drift higher and higher and felt himself floundering. A gust of wind shook him and he blinked heavily, looking at the creature, then his wife, then the dogs.

"The shed," he said finally. "Let's get to the shed," his voice was stronger the second time.

"How? The snow is so deep."

"Not on this side of the house. Luck was on our side with the roof collapse, the porch creates that wind pocket. Come on, let's get over there." He turned and pulled her out through the ruined front door, fist still held tight to his shirt. The snow right in front of the house was deep and creeping closer now that the second floor overhang was gone but there was enough of a path that they were able to make it around the side of the house. Harold hurried forward, turning sideways to get between the shed and the house so they could make it through the back door which was, thankfully, windswept clear of major snow piles. Sharon was puffing with exertion and behind her, the dogs were wading through chest deep snow. They were big but able to squeeze through the gap.

"Here Sharon, get in," he held the door for her and waited as the dogs filed before following the line and pulling the door shut.

And then they waited, crouched quietly in the shed as the snow whispered down around them and it got colder and darker. Just when Harold felt at his breaking point, Sharon and the dogs trembling with cold and fatigue beside him, the whisper of snow stopped. He raised his head and clutching the rifle tight, Harold stood and peered through a crack in the shed door. The night sky was covered with soot grey clouds but as he watched, patches began to appear, showing stars and clear sky. He felt hope bloom in his chest but sat back down and hugged Sharon close to him. There was still so much snow and he couldn't tell if there were any more *things* lurking outside.

By the time the sun rose, Harold and Sharon were miserable and stiff, Sharon nearly sobbing from the cold. Their dogs were a pitiful, shivering pile in their laps. When the faint rays of sunlight flooded the shed, Sharon raised her tear streaked face and let out a shaky breath.

"Do you think it's safe?" she whispered, her voice hoarse and trembling.

"I hope so, we have to chance it anyway," he replied, squeezing the hand she pushed into his. Groaning and blowing, the two of them shoved themselves to their feet and shuffled to the door. Harold kissed Sharon's hand and then dropped it so he could bring the rifle muzzle up. He used the barrel to push open the door but dropped it as he gaped in confused wonder as the sight outside. The sun was barely above the horizon, giving no warmth at all, yet where it's light fell the snow was rapidly melting. Rivers of freezing water were rushing through the yard and even where night still shaded the massive drift, he could see the glistening beginnings of melt.

"Wasn't the snow supposed to keep going? They said there would be days of it," Sharon said, her eyes darting everywhere.

"Well, they didn't forecast those monsters so I don't guess they know what this really is. Come on, let's see if we can get to the den. I don't think the second floor fell everywhere and we can get the fireplace going at least. Here," he helped her wade through a drift, "just follow right behind, nice and quiet. Just in case." He led them back the way they'd come the night before, this time through heavy snow that was rapidly turning to slush, and tried not to think of what they were going to do if they couldn't get warm soon. He couldn't see the cars, not yet, and didn't want to have to dig one out. He didn't know if there was anything hiding in the drifts.

They made it to the collapsed porch and into the house with no trouble. As they eased past the crushed creature, Harold heard Sharon let out a small gasp that she quickly stifled.

"Sorry! It's nothing," she hissed. "It's just…look!" She nodded down toward the creature which was exposed to the sunlight through the collapsed roof and, as they watched, it continued the process it had been going through; rapid degeneration, the skin and muscle and even bone and teeth collapsing into the floor.

"Like vampires," Harold said and then shook his head, annoyed at his own words, and pulled Sharon toward the back of the house. Luck continued to favor them, it seemed. The den was fine, dry and ready to be warmed by the large fireplace that dominated the back wall. They all piled in and Sharon shut the door before hurrying to the closet and digging through until she found their storage tubs full of thick blankets. She wrapped one around herself and piled more onto the dogs who had all gone to their dog beds and curled up. Harold got a fire going quickly and then they were huddled on the thick rug, wrapped in blankets and basking in the growing warmth baking toward them from the fireplace.

"Harold," Sharon started but then stopped and cleared her throat. "What the hell was all that? How could any of what happened—even be possible?"

"I don't know Sharon. I just—I don't know."

"Do you think it's really over?" She pushed closer into him as she asked and he kissed the top of her head.

"I hope so," he replied and he looked behind him at the door they'd quickly blockaded, just to be sure it was still shut fast. Outside, the sun was still burning the snow away and Harold shivered at the heat of the fire and the horror of what they'd just lived through.

The phone jangling in the uneasy silence made Harold jump and pulled a shrill, whispery scream from Sharon. Harold fumbled the phone from his pocket, astounded that it still had battery and wondering when they'd turned the ringer back on. It was Julianne.

"Honey? Hello? Are you okay?"

"Dad, we're okay. Oh my god." Julianne took a deep, trembling breath and let it out in one slow, measured breath which they could hear through the phone. "We're okay, the snow is melting here and the things are gone. Everyone says they're gone. You're alright there?"

"Yes, the snow is melting here as well. The house has fallen in, a lot of it fallen in, but we're okay. We have shelter and food and…we're fine here. Can you guys get home? Where's Scott?"

"He stayed home, he was feeling under the weather. I haven't been able to reach him but none of the landlines work and you know how awful he is for charging his cell." Harold heard the stress and anxiety in his daughter's forced chuckle; he knew how worried she was for her husband. "We're leaving now to go home. The car is totally uncovered and the snow is nearly melted here. I'll call you when we get home, okay?"

"Okay. We love you honey. Be careful on the drive home. You never know what might…you just never know." He finished awkwardly. Julianne told them she loved him and they could hear their grandson in the background shouting his own parting words and then line went blank and Harold was staring at the apps on his home screen.

"Do you think he's alright," Sharon asked quietly. "They don't have a basement or anything."

"We'll know soon enough," Harold answered grimly. He hauled himself up after a moment, keeping one blanket wrapped tightly around himself. Moving as quickly as he could with a stiff and cold body, he got water and food for the dogs, rummaging in the mostly intact cellar for things that he and Sharon to eat as well and then huddled back in front of the fire. As they ate cold peaches and beans, sharing bites with the dogs, Harold was struck by how quiet everything was. They were by no means close to a major highway or even to the nearest town yet he felt there was always some sort of sound happening outside, whether it was heavy duty farm trucks going past or even plows and tractors.

Today there was nothing but the crackle of the fire and the faint gurgle of melted snow traveling in thick rivulets through the yard.

A shocking burst of loud static below them made Harold and Sharon jump, Sharon loosing a tiny scream that she quickly bit back. The radio was going. They stared at each other, wide-eyed, as the breathless and panicked voice of the same radio dj from before began to cut through the silence.

"The snow is back! I repeat, the snow is back and we're already getting reports that it's worse than before. Ladies and gentlemen, this is not a joke or a drill or a prank or a whatever the hell. Listen, get somewhere deep and hide. The things are different, they're bigger and they're not going down as easy. There's no one coming this time folks, so please panic but do it responsibly. Get guns, get below decks, get..." his voice cut off with a shrill scream and the heavy sound of breaking glass and then it went dead.

"No, Harold. No, no, no." Sharon would have continued but Harold cut her off. He kissed her, hard, tried once to call his daughter but gave up when the signal wouldn't go through and then, before he could decide what to do, they both looked out the large window as clouds covered the yard and house in shadow. Both watched in desperate horror as the first flakes began to fall and the dogs, as one, began to softly whine.

Made in the USA
Columbia, SC
02 June 2025